LUKE'S LADY

Mara Fitzcharles

A KISMET® Romance

METEOR PUBLISHING CORPORATION
Bensalem, Pennsylvania

To Linda, who wanted Luke's story,
with love and special thanks for
sharing the laughter and the tears.

MARA FITZCHARLES

Born, raised, and educated in eastern Pennsylvania, Mara Fitzcharles now lives in northeastern Maryland, not quite deep enough in the woods or close enough to the water to satisfy her love of nature. In addition to reading and writing, she enjoys long walks, classical music, and traveling throughout the United States with her husband and four sons.

_____ PROLOGUE _____

Jess MacLaren rapped on the door to the tower room, then waited patiently for a response.

There was none.

He balled his fist and pounded against the wooden door, hoping Luke would answer before his parents were disturbed by the noise at the back of their house.

Still nothing.

"Luke! Open up!" As his patience diminished, Jess tried the glass knob and, when it turned easily in his hand, let himself into his brother's spacious apartment.

He couldn't help but notice the disarray. Luke never kept his quarters tidy. Today, however, the clutter was much worse than usual. Not one square inch had been spared. His first glimpse made him think the place was vacant. Then he spied a leather wallet and matching key case on the dresser, evidence his brother was there. Somewhere.

"Luke!" he called out.

"Yeah," came a muffled reply from the far corner.

Jess zeroed in on a large, rumpled heap sprawled across the bed. Long, jeans-clad legs tangled with the sheets and blankets, which half covered Luke's well-muscled form. A pillow flung sideways completely hid his head.

"What the devil is wrong with you?" Jess bellowed. "Why didn't you answer the door?"

Luke raised his head slightly and looked at his older brother in sleepy-eyed confusion. "Didn't hear you knock. I guess I drank more than I thought I did."

"You seldom have more than two or three social drinks—"

"Yeah," he acknowledged with a sort of shrug.

"And . . ." Jess prompted.

Luke's sigh was loud and long, his movements unhurried as he sat and swung his legs over the side of the bed.

"I had more than three," he mumbled.

"What's wrong?" Jess demanded. "You're not a drinker. What happened?"

Turning away, Luke slammed his fist into his pillow with such force that it bounced off the headboard and onto the floor.

"It fell apart, big brother. It all fell apart—"

"You aren't making sense," Jess pointed out.

"I'm not surprised," Luke said. "None of this makes sense."

Exasperated, Jess crossed to the desk, pulled out the chair, and seated himself. He noticed this side of the room, including Luke's work area, had also suffered abuse. "We'll take this slow, Luke. I'm afraid I don't understand why you were drinking—"

"Maggie," Luke whispered. Both syllables were laced with pain, as if being torn from him.

"You'd better tell me what happened," Jess said, studying Luke's anguished appearance. His gaze shifted to the total disarray in the tower room, focusing momentarily on a pile of shattered glass in the corner before returning to his younger brother. "I have the distinct feeling you're saying this wasn't a friendly little spat."

"No kiss and make love after this one. It's over," Luke groaned. "Damn!"

"Explain," Jess demanded.

"In your line of work, counselor, this is referred to as irreconcilable differences—"

"Bull!"

"Truth, big brother."

"You and Maggie have one of the best relationships going."

"Had. Past tense," Luke declared miserably.

"Something that good, that strong, doesn't end."

"Yeah," Luke conceded. "But we had a few . . . *weak* spots that damaged the structure of our fine, *strong* relationship."

"What?" Jess dared to ask. "What kind of weak spots?"

"Hey, lighten up. I'm not a client. I'm your brother. And as I see it, unmarried couples don't require any counseling to improve fractured relationships."

"Fractured? Not severed?"

"Semantics. My mistake, counselor. Maggie and I are severed. Damn!"

"Why?"

"I pushed," Luke admitted. "Guess I pushed too hard. Maggie bolted . . . split . . . as in good-bye."

"You're saying she's gone for good? She hasn't merely flown off somewhere for a few months?" Jess queried. "What the hell happened?"

"The weakest spot—" Luke forced out the words "—was our perennial debate over career versus commitment."

"The two of you always bandied that about. It was merely good-natured ribbing."

"No," he denied. "Oh, no. Good-natured on the surface, but underneath the currents were swift and strong. Behind closed doors, we argued."

His brother shot him a surprised glance.

"Truth."

Jess's brow furrowed as he considered the younger man. "I'm not buying it, Luke. You and Maggie smiled and laughed together. You loved each other. It was obvious to everyone."

"Yeah. Loved . . . past tense. I loved Maggie. Maggie loved me. But not enough, it seems, not enough. Imagine, Jess . . ." He paused, swallowing back strong emotions. "Imagine if you can, loving Brianna and not having her return your love."

"Maggie returned your love, you fool!"

"You're not seeing this from my side. Listen to me!" he insisted. "Maggie loved Luke, but I . . . put *her* first. I gave her freedom. She took off to Europe for six months to study. I waited. Then she wanted to get her doctorate. I said, 'Sure, honey,' and I waited."

Luke paused again, sending a pleading look to Jess, begging him to understand. "I love her. I want a wife, a home, a family . . . but I've postponed what I wanted because Maggie wanted . . . other things first." He sucked in a large breath, then let it out bit by bit.

"I got tired of waiting. While I sat back with our future in a holding pattern, I realized she may wait a lifetime and never achieve her goals. So I began to pressure her for a decision. I was tired of waiting in the wings, tired of playing the good guy." The flow of words halted and Luke closed his eyes in private agony.

His voice dropped when he continued. "I pushed too hard. I pushed her to decide . . . and she did, big brother. She did."

Again he stopped. For a minute only the quiet whoosh of Luke's defeated sigh sounded in the room.

"Maggie chose art . . . as if she thought our love, our marriage, would interfere with her dream. After all the freedom I gave her, all the time I gave her . . . after the love. . . ." His voice trailed off.

Admitting out loud he'd been rejected caused renewed distress, as strong and wrenching as physical pain. He sat on the edge of his bed, not only hurt, but puzzled and frustrated. At last he lifted his eyes to meet his brother's.

"She says she loves me, but she wants a career instead of marriage. Marriage and commitment would tie her down. Continuing our relationship would tie her down. . . ."

Luke lowered his head into his hands. "I don't know how to deal with the future. I've expected her to be part of it for so long."

"I'm sorry, Luke," Jess murmured. "I had no idea—"

"I tried to understand her," Luke continued. "I tried to see her side. Why the hell couldn't she compromise? Why? If she loves me, why did she do this?"

"She's dedicated to her painting. You know that. And, I suppose, she's driven by creative demons."

"And she doesn't need me?"

"You, little brother, beneath that carefree veneer, are a threat to Maggie."

"Me? A threat?" Luke echoed, tapping a thumb on his chest. "How can I be a threat? I've given her every ounce of freedom she's wanted."

"But consider your talent, Luke. You're already succeeding in a far corner of her world. You're part of the competition. Every success you have plays against her lack of success."

"Damn!" Luke exclaimed. "Maggie's always been happy with my success. What you're saying isn't possible. Why the hell should a portrait painter give a tinker's damn about how successful her architect lover is?''

"You've taken on quite a few prestigious offers. Big bucks. Recognition. *Success* in your own field."

"It's not the same! I can't paint faces. I don't want to!''

"I realize that,'' Jess said. "I was only playing devil's advocate. What if—''

"Well, mister advocate, I lose, whether your reasoning is correct or not. The painter in question has moved on. We cut clean. Good-bye.. Don't call. Don't write. I told her to be happy. . . .'' He faltered. "She smiled and said, 'Love ya, Luke.' ''

"It hurts like hell, so you decided to drown your sorrows.''

Luke shook his head. "No. I . . . trashed the room first.''

Jess gave him sort of a half smile. "I noticed it was a tad more cluttered than your usual haphazard decor.''

"Yeah,'' Luke drawled. "Guess I made a mess of the place.'' He paused, seeing the destruction now in the light of day. "I didn't know what to do. I hurt. Drew always yells when he's upset. It helps him. Rachel cries or stomps off and hides from the world.''

"That's not your style.'' Jess suppressed the urge to laugh at the mental picture of Luke retreating in hysterics like their younger sister.

"Smashing glassware isn't my style, either. I poured myself a drink.''

"That's not—'' Jess began.

"My style,'' Luke finished. "It's not . . .'' He rose to his feet and faced the window. "But in the back of my mind I remembered they used liquor to anesthetize soldiers during the Revolution.'' He shrugged, then rubbed the back of his neck as if he were world-weary.

"I don't know how well it worked for surgery, but it sure as hell didn't deaden my pain."

"It won't. If this is the end, Luke, only time will lessen what you're feeling." Jess inhaled deeply, wrestling with the helplessness of watching his brother suffer. "This may sound callous, but I'm going to say it in spite of the way it sounds. Perhaps you should find another woman. If you're careful, the aftereffects aren't quite as devastating as the scotch."

"I only want Maggie!"

"I'm trying to make helpful suggestions," Jess pointed out.

"Yeah. Well, I suggest you keep your helpfulness to yourself!"

"Have I ever been able to do that?" he countered. "You realize I ought to deliver a brotherly lecture on the evils of alcohol, not that I believe for one minute that you need it, but considering the present circumstance—"

"Hey, Jess," Luke interrupted. "There's still some scotch left. Why don't you take it home with you, if you're so damned concerned that I'll succumb to the power of the vile stuff?"

"Luke, you're hurting and vulnerable. Don't do anything foolish, anything you'll regret. And don't shut yourself off from us."

"End of lecture?" Luke asked hopefully.

"I hadn't even started," Jess informed him.

Luke held up his right hand. "I solemnly promise not to do anything I'll regret. No drunken binges . . ."

Jess cringed.

"No reckless involvement . . ." He faltered. "Say, Jess, maybe you could help me here. What else should I avoid?"

"I believe you have the right idea." Jess chuckled, half to himself. "By the way, I tried to call to invite you to dinner this evening. Your line was busy. It appears your phone took a direct hit during last night's skirmish."

Luke glanced in the general direction of the telephone. "This place is a mess," he groaned.

"Will you join us for dinner—" Jess paused and looked around the room— "after you restore order here?"

"Sure." Luke nodded twice. "I could use some company."

As soon as Jess left, Luke began the cleanup. But everything reminded him of Maggie—and the bombshell she'd dropped when he'd taken her home after dinner last night.

He thought himself a fool for not seeing it coming. In the past nine months she'd been out of the country more than she'd been home. And even when she was home, she repeatedly made excuses for neglecting their relationship. But knowing she loved him kept him contented.

Or had it? Perhaps that explained why he'd felt so restless and at the same time so determined to pressure Maggie for a commitment. Perhaps he'd realized on some level that she was pulling away from him.

Everyone had assumed things were fine between them. On the surface they had been. He loved Maggie and Maggie loved him—from a distance.

But he hadn't wanted a long-distance relationship. He'd tolerated it, believing he was giving her the opportunity to study and the freedom to pursue her dreams. He'd always expected to share them with her someday. He had never expected her to leave him. And he didn't know how to cope with the loneliness.

Jess had mentioned finding another woman. How could any other woman fill the emptiness?

Luke crossed the room to the closet. Gingerly taking

a long, slender tube from the shelf, he turned and emptied the contents onto his drawing table.

The plans to his dream house spilled out and, as he smoothed his hand over the paper, seemed to stare back at him, taunting him with a future that was lost.

Sadness engulfed him as his mind wandered through the rooms of the floor plan—the studio, the master bedroom, the nursery. . . .

Luke stopped himself before the emotion grew stronger. He rolled the paper into a cylinder, then shoved it back inside the tube.

An unexpected chill ran up his spine, and he realized he'd felt it before. It was an intense version of the way he'd felt each time Maggie took off to study somewhere, or disappointed him by forgetting to keep a date.

Maybe his wise older brother was right about finding another woman. Holding someone soft and warm and sweet-scented would be nice. But not just now.

Luke collapsed into an armchair and closed his eyes. Maybe the hurt would go away in time.

But not yet . . .

_____ ONE _____

Luke scanned the dimly lit, smoke-filled room once, then twice, searching for that nameless something or someone to help pass the time. Because time, he had concluded, was a crucial factor. Time passed and wounds healed. Therefore, all he needed was a pleasant way to help it pass. He needed a companion—a woman companion. And somewhere in Boston there had to be at least one who was lonely and willing.

Seconds later he spotted a solitary figure at a table not fifteen feet from the door. A woman. An attractive blonde. Her almost white hair was cropped quite short. Her large eyes focused on the twisted straw she held. For a moment he watched as slender fingers folded the straw in an intricate pattern, unfolded it, and began again.

Then his gaze moved on. She had delicate, feminine features: small pierced ears, dainty nose, full lips. She wore a navy tailored suit, white blouse, and a tie.

Not bad, he thought, in spite of the businesslike suit of armor. And different, too. Not dark and intense. No obvious similarities.

After another more thorough appraisal, he decided to buy her a drink and sauntered in her direction.

"What's a nice girl like you doing in a place like this?" he asked, leaning palms down on the table across from her.

She seemed cool, distant, indifferent to his presence as her eyes strayed toward the crowd at the bar. "I came with a friend," she said.

The warm, husky tone of her voice surprised him. It was incongruous with her appearance, but fascinating. He wanted her to continue.

"The brunette leaning on the bar?" he guessed.

A faint smile softened her face. "Yes, the brunette in the tight black skirt."

"She's latched on to someone else," he pointed out as a tall, athletic-looking man encircled the brunette's waist with his arm.

"So it seems," she acknowledged. "*I'm* not looking for company."

"Message received." He ran a finger over his mustache while he considered his options. He didn't want to be alone. He needed to be with someone. Her whisky-smooth voice enchanted him. "It's a shame to waste a table meant for four on one lonely lady. Mind if I join you?"

She sighed resignedly. "You may as well."

Luke pulled out the barrel-shaped chair and positioned himself facing her. He liked what he saw. She was easy on the eyes. . . .

"I'm Luke MacLaren." Reaching across the table, he offered his hand.

"Amanda Burke." Her eyes darted from him to the bar again as if she expected her friend to intervene. Then she extended her arm, accepting his handshake.

He noticed her fingers were delicate and feminine, her flesh soft and warm against his. Yet he was not surprised to find her handshake as firm and businesslike as her attire.

"Amanda Burke," he repeated, mulling over this piece of information. "Sounds familiar, but I'm afraid I can't place it."

"Amanda Burke and Amy Benson," she replied, nodding toward the bar. "Burke and Benson Realty."

"Ah! That's it!" he remembered. "One of your signs graces the street where I live."

"And where might that be?"

"Old residential section—"

"Dripping with old money?" Large aquamarine eyes opened wide, meeting his directly for the first time.

"My parents' home," he explained.

She stared at him, undisguised curiosity lighting her expressive face. "You live with your parents?" Her voice was heavy with disbelief.

"Not *with* them," he stressed to clarify his situation. "The Tower room has been converted to an apartment."

"But why?"

"Lighting is good there. It's comfortable. You know, homey. Anyway, I come and go as I please."

"Lighting?" she queried, obviously puzzled.

"Yeah." The corners of his mouth curved upward in amusement. "I'm an architect. Lighting is important. If I move out, I'll have a devil of a time finding a place to suit me."

"Okay." She smiled, responding to his amused grin. "As I tell my clients, whatever suits you. . . . It just seems strange to find a grown man still living at home."

"Family's close. I've had no reason to move," he stated simply.

She studied the virile-looking man seated across the table. He was being too casual about this. His posture was relaxed. He'd draped himself in the chair with the natural ease that stems from a laid-back nature. But she'd noticed a flicker of pain cross his face as he mentioned having no reason to move. And that devastating grin had not reached his eyes.

Beautiful, sad eyes, she thought. Murky, sea-green eyes right now. For a fleeting moment she wondered how those eyes would change when filled with passion. Then just as quickly, she smiled at herself for having such absurd thoughts.

"Amused?" he asked.

"Curious," she corrected.

"Yeah. I guess it sounds weird. I'm twenty-eight and I live in my parents' home."

Though he offered no further explanation, she wondered out loud, "Doesn't that cramp your style?"

She immediately regretted her forthright question. His handsome features froze and his eyes turned stormy.

"No," he said. "Doesn't cramp my style at all. Can I get you another drink?"

Mandy tilted her glass to stare at its contents. The remaining cubes clinked as they tumbled together. "Perrier," she replied.

"Nothing stronger?"

"No, thank you. Perrier is fine."

"Suit yourself." He turned away to summon the waiter and order their drinks.

She took the opportunity to admire his thick chestnut hair. It seemed to have a tendency to wave. She was sure he had struggled earlier to comb every curl until it appeared as straight as possible. Here and there, however, nature had triumphed over man's ministrations. She liked the overall effect. It fit the casual demeanor Luke MacLaren presented.

"Where were we?" He suddenly shifted his attention back to her. The waiter was nowhere in sight.

"Storm clouds were moving in. I believe I must have hit a nerve by questioning your lifestyle," she said.

Luke grinned, but he knew it was a halfhearted attempt at best. "Astute observation, Amanda Burke. Nerves are a bit raw these days. Open. Bleeding. I've joined the ranks of the walking wounded."

There had been a time or two he'd felt worse than wounded. But he didn't need to dump his sorrows on this beautiful lady. He just needed to *feel* less.

He glanced into the crowd, searching for the waiter, then returned his gaze to his companion. "My *lifestyle*," he explained, "remains unchanged in spite of the nerve damage."

He shrugged then, more to rid himself of unwanted memories than for any other reason. He'd come here to forget, not to parade his wounds in public. He couldn't change the way things were. Nothing could.

He spied the waiter across the room and watched his slow progress through the now-crowded bar. And when the man placed their drinks on the table, Luke muttered his thanks and paid him.

He reached for his, but as his hand closed around the glass, he paused, studying the dark amber liquid as if there were something unseen in it. Even if he searched for an eternity, he wouldn't find the answers he needed in this stuff.

Earlier he'd thought alcohol might offer a welcome respite from his troubles. But he knew the effect would be only temporary. And it wouldn't touch the heart of the matter. Loneliness and hurt couldn't be drowned so simply.

Or forgotten. That was the problem. He wanted to forget.

He loosened his grip on the glass and willed himself to shake off the threat of despair. He'd found a companion. Maybe she would help him forget. And the drink would quench his thirst.

As he lifted the glass to his mouth and took two successive gulps, he read disapproval in her wide-eyed stare.

"You don't approve of liquor?" he queried as he set his drink firmly on the table.

She shrugged. "Not really."

"If you don't like to see a guy take a drink, why the hell are you in a bar, lady?"

" 'What's a nice girl like me doing in a place like this?' " She tossed his earlier words back at him.

"Exactly."

"I told you. I came with a friend."

"She deserted you."

"Yes, it would appear as if she has deserted me. There are other reasons to come to bars, it seems. My friend's reason for example."

"Yeah," Luke acknowledged, nodding slowly. A hint of a smile tipped the corners of his mouth. "It was the *other* reasons that brought me here."

"Not the drink you couldn't wait to get your hands on?"

"Maybe, just a little," he confessed. "Although I've been told this is not the answer."

"Believe me," she advised, "that is *not* an answer. That stuff will destroy you."

"Voice of experience?"

One slender finger tapped the rim of her glass. "Yes."

"You don't look destroyed, lady."

She studied him for several moments, assessing the situation. "My friends call me Mandy."

"Mandy," he echoed. "Am I your friend?"

"I guess you are. I don't spill my guts to strangers."

"You haven't."

"No, but . . . I . . ." She hesitated. "Listen, Luke. I'd like to be honest with you. You gulped that drink almost like you couldn't go another minute without. Like it was a welcome friend."

"Back off," he muttered. He hadn't come here for a lecture.

"No," she insisted. "Hear me out. My father was an alcoholic—"

All at once she stopped, stunned. For the first time in her life she'd admitted that embarrassing bit of information out loud—and to a stranger. Here she was spilling her guts to a stranger because he had murky green eyes that seemed tormented.

She was only drinking Perrier, she realized. It didn't make sense.

"Mandy." His low voice was quiet, compassionate, as he ever so carefully removed her slender fingers from where they were clenched round her glass. He lifted her hand to enfold it in both of his.

Luke noticed her flesh felt cool now and pressed his palms tightly against her hand to take the chill away. He wanted, needed, to feel her warmth again.

"I'm *not* an alcoholic," he insisted, giving her a gentle squeeze. "I rarely drink." *Unless you count the past three weeks,* he thought. "This drink," he told her, "did seem like a lifeline, but only for a second. And tonight I have reason—"

"No!" she protested. "You can't let a drink be a lifeline. It's a foolish waste! Are you a good architect?"

"I am," he verified with a nod.

"When your mind's all fuzzy or your hands are shaking, you won't be! Don't do that to yourself, Luke."

"I wouldn't do that," he stressed. "I've told you I rarely drink. Besides, my brother already delivered lecture number one on temperance."

"It's obvious it didn't sink in and you need to hear it again," she snapped.

He shook his head and chuckled to himself. "Lighten up, lady. You're blowing this all out of proportion. I didn't come here to get drunk."

"You are drinking," she pointed out.

"I am, but it shouldn't be an issue."

"All right, then, why are you here?"

"For the same reason as your friend. My brother suggested I find a woman."

"Where is Amy, anyway?" Mandy asked, turning in her seat to search for her friend.

"She left with the blond jock," Luke answered with a nod toward the door.

"What?"

"I said—"

She cut him off. "I heard what you said. When did they leave?"

"A few minutes ago."

Mandy made an unladylike face. "She could have told me."

"I guess she assumed you were otherwise occupied," he volunteered, his tone sympathetic.

Compelled by the caring she sensed in his manner, Mandy stared at him. She forgot her annoyance with Amy Benson. Luke looked forlorn, like an abandoned child. Something about that little-boy look touched her. It was in direct contrast to their adult conversation. She smiled at the irony. "Otherwise occupied, huh?"

Amusement softened his features further. His expression brightened, developing into a full-blown smile. He shrugged his shoulders, raised his glass in a toast, then brought it to his mouth and took another large swallow.

"Yeah, well, you know what I mean," he teased.

"Yeah, well, I do," she mimicked, twirling the

straw in her Perrier. "So, Luke MacLaren, you didn't come here to drink, you came to socialize?"

"You might say I came to socialize," he replied, watching for her reaction. "My intentions weren't exactly pure, however. I specifically intended to find a willing woman."

She met his steady gaze head on. There was something about the way he looked at her—something that felt comfortable. Mandy fought to suppress the smile that was already curving the corners of her mouth. "A woman willing to do what?" she dared.

"Don't be cute, lady," he rasped. "I'm admitting I'm looking for a casual sexual encounter. Either you're interested or you're not. If not, I'll drive you home and that's that!"

"No strings? No involvement? Just a friendly roll in the hay?"

"Yeah."

"And if I'm not willing, you say you'll drive me home and ask nothing more?"

"Yeah," he repeated.

"Tempting," she replied, studying him once more. She liked the way he looked. She had been suckered by his sad eyes from the first. Yet even if she hadn't been, she couldn't deny he was attractive.

"Are you game?"

"How do I know you're not an ax murderer?" she challenged.

He rolled his eyes upward, then shot her a beguiling grin. "Blind faith?" he suggested, chuckling. "I'm not an ax murderer. My family wouldn't allow such unseemly, antisocial behavior."

Mandy mulled over her decision. She needed a ride. Amy had left her to her own devices. The choice was either Luke MacLaren or a cab. Luke seemed much more desirable than a cab.

Desirable, she mused. She found him far more than desirable. She sensed a kind of chemistry. His hands had been strong yet gentle when he'd touched her. And warm, so very warm. She'd felt his heat from her fingertips all the way deep inside, as if he'd touched her there somehow. It had been forever since she'd been warm inside, too.

Her eyes roamed deliberately over him. In her silence, he'd turned sideways, watching the crowded bar. As she studied his profile, she found herself responding to his physical appearance, overwhelmed by an unusual sensation in the pit of her stomach.

Just chemistry, she scoffed silently. She wiped the water beads from her glass of Perrier, then focused on Luke again. "Your place or mine?"

"Yours. I don't take women home," he reminded her.

" 'Course not," she murmured. Then, staring pointedly at his drink, she added, "You shouldn't be driving. . . ."

"No problem, lady. I'll hand over the keys and you can drive us to your apartment."

Luke stood quietly at Mandy's side as she struggled with the lock to her apartment door. When it finally gave, she pushed the door open and reached for the light switch. As the room was illuminated, he walked past her, into her domain, shrugging out of his coat and kicking off his shoes while he moved forward.

He scanned the room as he unfastened the buttons of his shirt. No surprises here. The furnishings were traditional—just what he'd expected from the business-like lady in the tailored suit. Not only traditional, but symmetrical. Matching tables on either side of the beige sofa held identical brass lamps. A toast-brown pillow graced each corner of the couch. Two very traditional overstuffed chairs, with a third table between them, balanced the other side of the room. The wall-to-wall carpeting was a creamy white.

Lord, he thought, *this place is almost sterile.*

Tugging his shirt free from his pants, he turned and glanced toward the kitchen. No surprises there, either. Gleaming white countertops. Spotless. A cinnamon-colored tablecloth covered the small dinette table. Sitting dead center was a brass pot filled with dried flowers.

He turned to face Mandy. She was standing, stock-still, in front of the closed apartment door. She hadn't budged an inch the entire time he'd made himself comfortable and surveyed his surroundings.

"You actually live here? This place is immaculate!"

"I live here," she responded woodenly.

"There were six of us growing up. Mom could never seem to make our home look picture-perfect with all of us and our friends cluttering the place. And now the grandchildren leave their paths of destruction. This is amazing!"

"I'm all alone," she said quietly.

Her words echoed his earlier thoughts, and something in her soft, husky tone touched him, warming him like fine brandy and a blazing fire on a blustery winter night. He paused and looked at her, really looked at her. He saw more than a willing body. More than a substitute for liquor or a painful memory. He saw a woman whose vulnerability was neatly disguised beneath her tailored suit but, for that fleeting moment, exposed in her expressive face.

Luke MacLaren was not an unfeeling man.

"Come here." He whispered his command and opened his arms to welcome her. "Tonight you won't be alone. Tonight neither of us will be lonely."

In a slow forward motion, Mandy crossed the space

between them and allowed herself to be engulfed by his warm, welcoming embrace. He held her close, his arms like bands of strength around her.

"Luke," she confessed, "I'm kind of new at this—"

"Christ, Mandy," he groaned into her hair. "This is not the time to tell me you're a virgin."

"Hardly," she whispered. "But I haven't been with anyone since my divorce." It seemed to her as if Luke's grip lessened just a bit.

For a minute they were both silent, sharing only their mutual need for warmth.

Then Luke released a long sigh. "No strings, no involvement, and no confessions . . . agreed?" he suggested, suppressing his own guilty feelings.

She nodded. "Fine."

He lifted her chin and cupped her face in his hands. His eyes shuttered closed before he lowered his head. All at once he felt her tense, felt her draw back slightly.

"Easy," he murmured, tunneling his fingers through her short, thick hair. "Easy. Just a kiss, Mandy." He coaxed her head closer. "One sweet kiss . . ."

Warm lips brushed across Mandy's mouth, softly, tenderly, tentatively, then all at once claimed it outright.

She never had a chance to check for storm clouds. Perhaps she should have. What began as a simple kiss escalated into a fiery, tumultuous act of passion. Neither of them could explain what happened when their lips touched. They were swept into a maelstrom and out of control.

Luke never broke contact with her, yet with unbelievable swiftness, he removed her clothing and the remainder of his, all the while pressing deliberately provocative kisses across her heated flesh. The way his hands slid over her silken skin left no doubt about his urgency or intent. One strong but gentle hand outlined the circle of her breast, tantalizing. The other seared a fiery path along her spine, settling intimately at the base, caressing her, urging her ever closer.

As he cradled her against his hips, a soft moan escaped from her. He covered her mouth hungrily with his, needing her warmth and taking it, yet in his own way giving more than pleasure to her aroused body.

Mandy felt a burning sweetness deep within. She realized in the heat of their passion he'd taken the time to protect her. All her doubts faded into mindless oblivion as he plied her mouth with tender kisses. When he moved to her chin, then her neck and her shoulders, she squirmed against him, digging her fingers into his wavy hair. As his tongue laved her sensitive nipples, she cried out his name.

"Now," he responded, pulling her to the floor with him. "Now, Mandy," he groaned as he eased himself inside her.

She was engulfed in the heat of desire as his hardness filled her, charging her with an electricity she had never before experienced. She abandoned herself to the blaze of passion exploding within. Nothing mattered, nothing existed except here and now. And here and now incredible sensations were coursing through her body. And through his. These feelings were shared. There was no doubt in her mind. One person could not feel this ecstasy alone. They were feeding off the passion of each other, soaring together. Together, until their passion was spent.

Luke lay on his back in the soft light of early morning, one arm pinned to the bed by the woman lying next to him. He smiled contentedly as he studied her naked body. Long, lean legs that had wrapped around him repeatedly throughout the night. Small hips, firm, flat stomach, full breasts, and the face of an angel—a beautiful, blond angel who'd shared herself with him, for whatever reason. His smile broadened as he scanned the room.

Her bedroom would have been a surprise if he had seen it last night before the passion was unleashed. But this morning, after the revealing hours they had passed together, he was not at all surprised. The room was ultrafeminine. White, with touches of mauve. Lacy. And, yes, picture-perfect, except for the very rumpled bed.

He decided the lady wore armor. And she had shed it for him. For a moment, he wondered why. Not that it mattered. They'd agreed not to make confessions. He was pleased with the outcome.

"Why are you smiling so deliciously? Did I actually satisfy the hungry animal?" Mandy's husky voice broke through his thoughts.

"You did, but that's not why I'm smiling," he replied, rolling on top of her. As he lowered his body against hers, he watched her eyes, eager to see her reaction. And when he recognized desire, he took possession of her mouth, seeking that elusive need she'd assuaged during the night.

Sighing against her soft lips, he groaned his contentment and murmured, "Good morning."

"You're insatiable," she whispered.

"I am," he agreed, parting her legs with his knee. "Are you complaining?"

"No. Oh, no. Luke," she cried, giving in to the desire sweeping through her.

And when he thrust into her a few moments later, their passion swiftly spiraled to heights Mandy had never believed attainable. Even in the aftermath, he continued exploring her flesh, delighting her, murmuring playful nothings in her ear.

"Do you always wake up that eager?" she whispered.

"Do you always neglect a proper 'Good morning'?" he countered, nibbling on her earlobe.

"I asked first," she reminded him.

"I'm waiting to hear 'Good morning.' "

"I gave you my body."

"No," he quipped. "We shared."

"Yes," she admitted, stretching to kiss him deeply and without restraint. "We shared."

"Well . . ." he prompted.

" 'Morning, Luke."

"Good?"

"Good? The morning? I suppose it's good," she explained. "I had the most fantastic lover last night—"

He smiled down at her. "Enjoyed him, did you?"

"Most definitely."

"Would you want to sleep with this guy again?"

"Sleep with him? Oh no. I didn't sleep much," she teased. One slender finger traced the outline of his mustache. "We, um, were otherwise occupied."

Luke slid his hands to her hips and held her as if staking a claim. "And would you like a repeat performance?"

"Most definitely."

"Same rules?" he suggested, watching her expressive face as he massaged the small of her back with his fingers. He was pleased by what he read there. She was so responsive to him. Even now.

"No strings?" Mandy's question sounded more like a groan of approval.

"Yeah—"

Her hands covered his suddenly, halting his words as well as his tantalizing massage. "Listen, Luke, you said no confessions. Agreed for now . . . except just this one. I had a lousy marriage. I've sworn off commitment. I've written off relationships, too. It's been a long time. . . ." She bit her lip, hedging.

"Yeah, you admitted that last night. Before," he reminded her.

She lifted her gaze to meet his directly. "If last night was your idea of casual sex, I'd be willing to repeat the performance."

"Tonight?"

"Tonight?" she echoed, more than a tinge of surprise evident in her voice.

"Just a suggestion, not a necessity," he returned. "I need what you gave me. Not just the sex, but the feel of your warmth in my arms during the night. I can tell you right now, I'd like to be with you again. . . . It's your decision."

"Tonight," she replied, releasing his hands to nudge a wayward lock of hair from his forehead.

After he left, Mandy stood in the quiet of her apartment, arms wrapped around herself, remembering the previous evening. Everywhere she looked there were little pieces of memory. What on earth had come over her? She had never, ever allowed herself to be picked up in a bar! The man was a definite hunk, but even so . . . She had invited a total stranger into her home, her bed, and worst of all, her body.

She wasn't like that. Not at all. Since her divorce she had kept to herself. She had a small circle of friends whom she loved and trusted, but she wasn't inclined to socialize with anyone outside those special few. So why did she do what she did?

She thought back to last night. He had joined her for a drink. That was innocent enough. They had chatted easily. Conversation had come naturally. She'd liked him. That was it. She had liked him right off, and accepted him. He'd displayed a kind of openness, an honesty she appreciated. He'd admitted he was looking for a woman. And later, much later, he'd told her he needed her warmth. That was some confession coming from a man.

He was a handsome brute, too. Above-average height, broad-shouldered, muscle-bound. Strong jaw. Great smile. Very kissable lips. She even liked his mustache. In the sunlight this morning she had seen the auburn highlights dancing in his chestnut brown hair. His deep-set eyes were, without a doubt, compelling. Such changeable, emotion-filled eyes.

She'd seen the hurt there and sensed his deeper, unspoken needs without realizing it at the time. She'd responded to the hidden part of him, knowing somehow he was wounded and required special care and compassion. Then she'd gone a bit further than necessary with her response.

He'd wanted a willing woman. Well, she certainly had proven herself willing! And, fool that she was, she'd do it again.

Why, though? Physical attraction? She had admired men before without being tempted to hop into bed with them after a few hours' acquaintance. Chemistry? He'd certainly started some sort of reaction inside her when his fingers touched hers. And that first kiss had been like none other she'd ever experienced. She'd careened out of control, somewhere beyond the realm of the known. Somewhere unbelievable and strangely comforting.

She assumed Luke MacLaren only wanted to scratch an itch. When it was satisfied, he would move on. This liaison would be temporary, fleeting.

Maybe that had its own appeal. She didn't care for involvement. Getting involved with another human being would inevitably bring hurt. And she had had enough involvement, enough hurt—enough for her lifetime. Never again would she be hurt. Never again would she allow herself to love any human being deeply.

Luke wanted a warm, willing body, good times,

good sex. Well, so did she. Good times, no strings. That's what had its appeal. She'd been cold forever. She wanted to feel warm again, too.

She felt a tad guilty, though, because she had been so easy, so wanton. That really was not at all the norm. Thank heaven he'd had enough good sense to be careful. What a mess she could have made of her life—again!

Mandy's gaze dropped to the carpet and riveted on the place where he had taken her, so swiftly, so completely out of control. That it had been beautiful and fulfilling astounded her. Casual sex, he'd termed it. No way was this casual. And no way was she fool enough to deny herself the pleasure of his body after the pain she had experienced. She had accepted his offer, determined to enjoy whatever "pleasure" life was about to toss her way.

Then she realized where her musings had taken her, not simply back to the previous night, but into herself, facing her own basic, forgotten needs. She couldn't point her finger and say exactly why she had given herself to him. It wasn't merely physical attraction, compassion, chemistry, or need. It was a combination of those things, wrapped tidily in a package labeled "Luke MacLaren."

For now she held the package.

TWO

It was almost ten o'clock when she heard the light rap on the door. She had showered and slipped into a silky blue caftan much earlier, not knowing if, or when, Luke would come. Now she set aside the quilting square she'd been working and hurried to answer the door.

She was apprehensive only until she opened it. His smile seemed so comfortable, so familiar, that Mandy was immediately at ease with him. She waved him in and, as she turned to lock the door, saw his hand already working to free the buttons of his shirt.

Amused, Mandy watched him tug the shirt with one hand and, with amazing dexterity, begin to remove his pants with the other. Her gaze never left Luke MacLaren's tall, lean body. She was fascinated by every provocative movement.

His eyes were on her, too. As he shed his shirt, he murmured, "Hi." Though he spoke just that one word, his voice was deep and smooth. Compelling. She felt her need for him rising and fought to keep herself from making the first move.

"Come here, Mandy," he ordered, stepping out of his pants mere seconds before he reached to enfold her in his arms.

"Eager, Luke?" she teased. Already his busy hands were caressing her, sending sparks of electricity shooting through her, warming her with an inexplicable intensity and causing that unusual sensation in the pit of her stomach and lower.

"You feel good," he groaned against her lips. "Soft. Inviting." His searching fingers found the small of her back, pressing her intimately against his aroused form. Then, with one sure movement, he swept her into his arms and strode to the bedroom.

His kisses were rapid and frenzied as he removed her caftan and lowered her beneath him on the bed. His mouth clung hungrily to hers, sipping, tasting, and making silent promises of the fulfillment to come. Gentle fingers tugged at her taut nipples, causing desire to spiral wildly within. She wanted him so much she thought he could not take her soon enough. She knew only minutes had passed, yet he aroused her with such speed and to such heights she could not wait another second.

Just as she opened her mouth to ask, he nudged her thighs apart and she wound her legs around his waist, urging him to lower his lean body.

Desperate to feel more of him, she touched his heated flesh, first kneading his shoulders and exploring the long, muscled back with her fingertips, then grasping his buttocks to invite him to her.

But Luke needed no invitation. He brought them together with exquisite mastery. As if they were two pieces of a puzzle perfectly joined, their union began.

Mandy knew the sweet ecstasy of sharing this physical act with him. She could feel her life's blood pulsing in every inch of her body and feel the rapid, heavy thud of Luke's heart where their flesh met. As he whispered words of passion and increased the pace of their union, she soared into the heavens—hot, explosive, out of control.

Afterward she was suspended somewhere between ecstasy and reality, barely aware of the comforter being pulled up and tucked around her, of the dampness of their sated bodies cocooned beneath the covers, or of the deep, rapid breathing of the man who was still joined with her.

She felt the low rumble of his words, as her head lay on his chest, before her mind registered what he said.

"You're good for me, Mandy."

His voice was quiet and calm. But Mandy sensed more than she heard in his words. Maybe their intimacy had sharpened her senses and given her a special knowledge of him. She knew he was using her, but didn't know why. Yet she recognized honesty in his admission.

At the same time she remembered their no-strings agreement. That was what she wanted, nothing more. In spite of the intensity of their physical actions, she needed to keep distance between them.

"Enjoyed yourself?" she queried, keeping her voice light as she peeked at him.

A smile lit his handsome face. She noticed this time his eyes were almost smiling, too.

"Yeah, I enjoyed myself." He rained moist, sweet kisses in an arc across her forehead. "The pleasure wasn't all mine, though, lady."

It would have been impossible to deny what she knew they both realized. "No," she acknowledged, sighing.

Mandy's sigh was captured by a kiss. And when the kiss was broken, his eyes mirrored her own questions.

"You are incredible!" He enunciated each whispered word.

"Good sex?" Mandy guessed, certain he could mean nothing else.

"Surprising."

"Oh?"

"Oh, yourself," he chuckled.

"Explain, MacLaren. That was a very curious remark," she pointed out. "Exactly why are you so surprised that . . . sex with me is—"

"As satisfying and beautiful as we both know it is," he finished for her. He trailed his finger along the side of her face and under her chin. His lips pursed thoughtfully.

"Did you ever get one of those specially gift-wrapped birthday presents . . . the kind you bring home from a department store. Looks good. Except you don't expect it to be what you really want?" He paused, waiting for her to answer, and when she nodded, he continued. "Then you unwrap the present and, wow! It explodes—shoots stars out at you. Incredible! Lady, you are incredible. That tailored business suit is nothing more than window-dressing. A costume. The lady underneath, the one in the lacy underwear, is so much woman, so exciting, I feel like, well, I've won a prize."

One finger traced the outline of her pert little nose, touching with a caress as light as a whisper, then moved to furrow her soft hair.

"I didn't say that well, did I? Women aren't possessions. Boy oh boy, do I know that!" he grumbled, scowling. "I'm not good at putting feelings into words, Mandy. You are not a present or a prize or an object. That's not what I meant. As far as intangibles go, being with you, like we've just been . . . well, I need . . . I need that particular feeling right now."

"Would you like to talk about it?" she inquired, reaching to rub his strong jaw with her fingertips.

His smile was full of apology. "We agreed no confessions."

"They're good for the soul."

"You're good for my soul," he chuckled as he gave her an affectionate squeeze. "And my ego, and my psyche—"

"Tell me, Luke," she coaxed all of a sudden. She decided she wanted to know, needed to know what lay hidden behind his sad eyes.

"Yeah, well," he hedged, shrugging. "Same old story. Little boy loses his favorite toy."

"Yeah, well, Luke," she chided softly, "toys can be replaced. The hurt I've seen in your eyes wasn't caused by the loss of a beloved toy."

"Right," he mumbled.

"Tell me," she encouraged. "Let the healing begin."

"You don't want to get me started. I'll get boring. Morose. Maudlin."

"I'll interrupt you with my delightful bedroom gymnastics if you get maudlin," she quipped, stretching one long leg into the air for emphasis. "Now, spill it, MacLaren." She poked her finger at his chest.

He closed his eyes and turned his head away, as if to shut her out. He seemed pensive, withdrawn. She knew she had pushed too far. Although she regretted her actions, she was unsure how to apologize without making matters worse.

For a while they lay in silence. When he sighed, she felt the slight tremor that shook his body. She reached up again, this time to smooth the thick, unruly locks of hair behind his ear. In response she felt the steel band of his arm tug her closer.

"I lost my lady," he rasped. "My lady. My life . . ." His tortured voice broke. "She didn't . . . want me."

Mandy felt him swallow, fighting back emotions that must have surfaced against his will.

"Married?" She had to ask. She needed to know that, too.

"Married?" he bit out. "Hell, no. I wanted marriage. Babies. All of it. My lady didn't. She wanted freedom. A career. No marriage, no ties, no Luke. Nothing . . . just nothing. Damn! How can you just turn off love, like a switch? How can you do that?" His voice rose, raw with frustration and confusion. It touched a nerve in Mandy.

"No one can turn it off and on," she emphasized. "Some people love more intensely. Some people give more freely and more completely. There are degrees of involvement."

"Yeah, well, I was fool enough to give, without question, because I loved her. I gave her all I could. Everything. Our world seemed perfect—until I expressed my desires."

"She didn't give in return?" Mandy probed, trying to keep both her words and her manner gentle.

"In retrospect, minimally."

"You wanted commitment. She didn't. You need sharing, give and take, to make a commitment. Some people only know how to take."

"That sounds like firsthand knowledge, Mandy."

"It is," she admitted. "My husband was a taker. I wasn't capable of giving as much as he . . . wanted from me. So, I became history."

"I know the feeling," Luke said, his voice heavy with defeat. "I'm history, too."

"We're both getting maudlin. Two losers lying together, feeling sorry for themselves. How depressing!" She walked her fingertips, inch by provocative inch, up the length of his thigh and across his hip bone to trace circles around his navel. "We can do better, can't we?" she asked coquettishly as her hand slid lower.

With the first tantalizing trail of her fingers, Luke's skin became sensitized to the warmth of her silken flesh touching his. He was aroused. He wanted her, needed her beyond belief, although it had been only a short time since their previous coupling.

"Incredible," he breathed. Capturing her mouth beneath his, he rolled on top of her, his pulse racing at breakneck speed. "Incredible, lady," he repeated as their passion grew and began to spiral once more toward the apex of ecstasy.

Mandy stormed into her apartment, slamming the door in her wake. She dumped her leather briefcase on the floor, kicked off her high-heeled shoes one at a time, and slipped out of her dove-gray suit coat, dropping it onto a nearby chair. She tugged open the hidden hooks of her green blouse and pushed the power button on her stereo. Tonight she wanted music—something, anything—to keep her company.

The room filled with the lazy sound of a jazz saxophone, which reminded her, in an odd way, of Luke MacLaren and his casual, yet intense nature.

She realized that shared nights had flowed into weeks. He'd been there with her more than he was not. So often, in fact, that she'd given him her extra key. Each time he let himself in, he appeared as eager as the first time, his pants unzipped by the time the door was shut and locked.

Each time she welcomed him. Luke was her own private, very special secret. Shut away in her room, locked in his arms, she was free to soar with him. He never failed to satisfy her physical desires. He was a gentle and thorough lover. And she knew he was always contented afterward.

They shared, each giving, each taking, each fulfilled.

Mandy had acknowledged their masks from the beginning. For each, the mask served a purpose. As time passed, she learned the man who held her tenderly within his arms while they slept was a sensitive, deeply caring individual whose casual veneer served to hide the depths of his dreams and his feelings.

Her own mask had been constructed, layer by layer, as each new assault ripped through her. Now, two short years after the last wound, with the layers of her facade firmly in place, she was able to present herself to the world as a composed, successful businesswoman. Except for a few close friends, no one ever knew or suspected otherwise. Amanda Burke had direction and purpose to her life—or so it appeared to others.

She suspected Luke's layers were thinner and newer. And she empathized with him. The things humans do to cover their pain and frustrations! She knew sharing was always better, but since Ben's death, there had been no one to share with. That was why she'd encouraged Luke to "spill it." That was why she always encouraged him to talk—after their sexual encounters, of course.

She knew him well enough to realize that when he said he needed her that was exactly what he meant. His needs were met and satisfied before no more than a half-dozen words were ever exchanged. His needs were the same as hers.

Some evenings her tension mounted to unbearable heights by the time he arrived and sated her. This was undoubtedly a two-way relationship, each of them equal partners, supplying what the other needed.

As the subtle music of the sax wrapped her in its embrace, she wished Luke's arms were holding her now. The too-long day caught up with her, swamping her with weariness that made her giddy. Stepping out of her skirt, she began to giggle like a schoolgirl.

Maybe it was the rhythm of the music inciting some heretofore unacknowledged primal instincts. Or maybe it was the realization that hit her as she stood, for the moment it took to wiggle out of her pantyhose, surveying the trail of belongings she'd left in her wake. "I'm picking up Luke's bad habits," she grumbled.

Again she wished for the warmth she found with him. Tonight of all nights the apartment was empty. She needed him. Not just the warmth, but his caring touch. She needed—

The music changed tempo. Mandy glanced at her pantyhose, then, on an impulse, rolled them into a ball and aimed at the brass lamp.

"Take that, world!" she muttered, pitching the make-shift ball into the air.

It came undone, missing the intended target by more than a foot. The hose fell, opened, onto the plush carpet. Mandy freed the catch of the bra as she watched the nylons land. Then she swung the intimate apparel around her finger until it sailed off into the air.

"Lord, I'm tired," she muttered as she stumbled into her dark bedroom, trying to remove her lace panties as she went. When she managed to step out of them, she left them on the floor.

At last, she collapsed gratefully, and none too gently, onto the hard mattress of her bed.

"Bad day?" a low, rumbling voice greeted her.

"Omigod, Luke!" she cried out. "You scared me! I had no idea you were here. Where are your clothes?"

"Neatly folded on yonder chair," he replied, laughing. "You weren't home. I had time to pick up after myself. Come over here, lady. I was lonely without you," he groaned, pulling her into his arms.

"I need you," she whispered against his mouth. "Tonight, Luke, I need you more than—"

Not giving her a chance to finish, he swiftly set about satisfying the need she had expressed. He soothed her with gentle, masterful caresses, then joined with her until her need was met and completely assuaged.

In the aftermath of their passionate encounter, he cradled her next to him as always. "Talk," he ordered, his voice low and quiet. "Tell me why this beautiful body is so racked with tension. If you're a good girl, Mandy, I just might reward you," he teased.

"How?" she murmured.

"I'll fulfill every erotic fantasy you've ever dreamed."

"That's been done," she said.

He laughed. Really laughed. His body shook so hard she bounced up and down against him.

"Talk," he commanded with mock sternness. "I have a friend who claims it's good for the soul."

"We are friends, aren't we?"

"Yeah, we're friends," he agreed, giving her an affectionate squeeze, then a brotherly kiss on the forehead. "And friends share bad days. Spill your guts, Amanda Burke."

"It was a long day," she told him. "One grumpy client monopolized the entire morning, then caught me this evening as I was about to leave the office. He wanted a contract drawn up and signed. I just finished with him. He had to be Ebenezer Scrooge's first cousin. He was impossible to please!"

"But you managed to do just that?"

She sighed a long, exasperated sigh. "Yeah. I think I did, but it took forever."

"Yeah," he mocked. "Now tell old Luke what's really wrong. You handle clients like that every day without letting them get under your skin. Today shouldn't be any different."

"What makes you think today is different?" she asked curiously. "You aren't usually here when I come home after a long, tiring day."

"Lady," he growled, "you have never been this tense. Never. Not even the first time, Mandy. Not even when you gave yourself to a total stranger."

"I'm not tense," she lied.

"Hey! Where's the honesty you always display?" he scolded, reaching for the bedside lamp. A soft glow illuminated the room when the light came on. "It's me, Luke, the lover you've been sharing your tense body with. That body, beautiful lady, doesn't lie to me. And neither should you." He pulled her on top of him, stroking her face with his fingers. "Talk to me," he whispered against her mouth.

His lips brushed over hers, back and forth, again and again. Mandy couldn't stand the torment. She took. She had to feel them pressing into her. She forced his head forward with her hand and fastened her lips to his, sucking, nibbling, demanding satisfaction.

"No more," he growled, breaking away from the embrace. "Talk."

"I need you," she whispered with a plea in her voice.

"I'm right here," he assured her. "Tell me what's wrong."

Mandy shook her head. "It won't help. There's nothing you can do."

"I can listen."

"Big deal," she said sarcastically.

"Did Ebenezer's cousin make a pass at you?"

She laughed ever so briefly. "No, nothing like that. He only pushed me to the point of frustration."

"I'm waiting." The words were spoken with calm, quiet emphasis.

"I'm . . . hurting," she revealed in a faint, choked

whisper. "It's an old wound, not a fresh one. Trouble is, it cut deep."

Even before her voice broke, Luke felt her trembling. "Today . . . the reminders. . . . Today . . . Oh, Luke, hold me please," she entreated.

"I am, sweet angel," he murmured, kissing her tears away. "I won't let you alone. I'll be here with you."

She cried softly in his arms for a few minutes. As she quieted, he felt her body relax. She snuggled against him, resting her head on his shoulder. Luke felt her need as if it were his own. He wanted to remove her burden, whatever it was, and carry it for her. That subtle realization made him feel as close to her as he had when they'd made love.

He cupped her chin in his hand and gazed into her tear-filled eyes. "Friends share," he reminded her.

She bobbed her head and he watched her swallow back the tears.

"You've mentioned brothers," she whispered. "How many do you have?"

"Three brothers. Two sisters."

"I had . . . I had only one brother," she said. "He died. Cancer. Three years ago . . . today."

"I'm sorry, Mandy. I wish I could have been there for you."

"Thank you. That's sweet," she acknowledged. "Ben was always there for me. When my father was drunk, in one of his frequent rages, Ben always sheltered me, protected me. Whenever I needed someone to talk to, he was there to listen. I tried to be there for him, too. When he got sick—" She stopped and shivered as she remembered the tortured look that had distorted her brother's handsome face. "He was in agony. Painkillers didn't help. He called me his sunshine, forced me to smile for him. I tried to be with him. His death left an unbelievable void in my life."

"Like a part of you is missing?" Luke guessed.

"How did you know?"

"My older brother says that's how he felt after an automobile accident brought him near death's door. I've felt his hurt. I've shared his misery. I can only imagine how I would feel if we had lost him or any of the others."

"Is your family close?"

"Emotionally, yes. Geographically, not always."

"I meant emotionally. You're fortunate to have that. Ben and I were close. My mother died when I was small. I don't remember her. My father never did anything to foster memories. Sometimes I like to think he started drinking to forget her, but I honestly don't know. All I know is that he was an angry, uncompromising drunk. I was afraid of him. And until I got married, Ben was the only person I cared about and the only one who cared about me."

"I grew up in the big house I still live in," Luke told her. "Everyone loved everyone else. Still do. We fought with one another, but we laughed and teased and played and shared. My feelings about growing up are happy, warm, safe feelings. My parents either love each other very much or they're award-winning actors. Each of us has always known how loved we are, just because we belong to them. I have trouble imagining how it must feel to be a child and not be loved by your family."

"Ben made the difference in my life," Mandy explained. "He loved me unconditionally, because I was his sister, for no other reason. We grew so close, so very close. I was his sunshine and he was the cement that held my world together."

"Then he was gone. . . ."

"Right." The word was spoken faintly, as if saying it any louder would mean risking more hurt.

Luke felt a strong tug of compassion even though his own family was still, thankfully, in tact. "You were married then, weren't you?" he asked.

"Yes, but my marriage couldn't begin to fill the void my brother's death created."

Luke shook his head. "I meant that at least you had your husband to lean on while you lived through the desolation of losing your brother. Surely it was better to share your grief with him than to suffer alone."

"I didn't think a grown man could possibly be as naive as you are." An odd emotion weighted her words, making her sound uncharacteristically impatient. "My husband was an only child who had never lost a loved one," she explained. "He couldn't understand my grief and did little to ease my distress."

"Sorry," he apologized. "You've never talked about your marriage. I had no idea. Contrary to what you believe, though, I realized a few years ago that not all marriages are made in heaven."

"Mine certainly wasn't," she muttered.

"Care to tell me about it?" he suggested. "Ole Luke's shoulder is good for crying on."

"So I have recently discovered."

"And you thought I was only good for sex!" he teased. "All this time you didn't know this body of mine had a dual purpose."

"Never even suspected it, old man," she admitted, poking him with her fingertip. "Maybe you shouldn't be so free with that information. Some women might be inclined to take advantage of those broad shoulders."

"Anytime," he offered. "I've had lots of practice. Two sisters, a sister-in-law, and a spunky little nephew have previously availed themselves of my services, in case you need references."

"Not necessary. I'm sure your, um, services are more than adequate."

He chuckled. "Okay, lady. I think I'll let that one pass. Feel free to end this meaningless chatter any time and get to the good stuff."

"The good stuff?" she teased, running one slender finger along his breast bone.

He grabbed at her hand and caught it in his. "Yeah," he growled, "confession is good for the soul."

"You want some cocoa?" she asked innocently.

"As a matter of fact," he told her, "I think cocoa would make a terrific midnight snack. Do you have any cookies?"

She shook her head. "Chocolate doughnuts?"

"All right! Junk food and true confessions!"

"You're crazy!" she laughed, reaching for her robe.

"Hey, lady . . ."

The sudden change in the tone of Luke's low rumble stopped her hand in midair.

"Forget the robe. You look fine."

Mandy turned. Astonished aquamarine eyes met with hazy sea green, locked in a silent, knowing exchange.

"Decadent," she whispered.

"Immoral," he added.

"Lewd."

"Lascivious."

"Lecherous."

"Salacious."

"Sexy."

"Cocoa."

"Yeah. Cocoa," she echoed.

A few minutes later they were seated in the kitchen dunking doughnuts into mugs of steaming cocoa.

"How old were you when you married?" Luke queried.

"Ah, time for the confessions." She licked chocolate icing from her fingers. "I was eighteen."

"Awfully young," he remarked, sounding more judgmental than usual.

"Too young to be making the decision of a lifetime," she agreed. "But there were . . . considerations."

"To bed or not to bed?" he asked candidly.

Surprised, she glanced up at him. "No, that's not what I meant. Living with my father's alcoholic rages was more than a little unpleasant. David offered me security, a future, and, most of all, an alternate lifestyle, a way out from under the tyranny of the drunkard. I took it. It was that simple."

"You married him to get out of your father's house? No affection?"

"Well, there was some in the beginning." She sighed. "David never had to share anything as a child. He never learned to share as an adult. If I needed to unload bad days, Ben was my sounding board. David had an old-fashioned 'you're the little woman' outlook. 'I'll provide, you obey.' I was only a kid, so I went along with it. I thought I loved him. He was a damn sight easier to live with than my father. A good provider but a lousy choice for a lifetime partner.

"I guess I realized that for the first time when my brother got sick. David couldn't understand my compulsion to help Ben, to be with him. Other people's needs weren't part of his vocabulary. Ben needed me and I needed to be with my dying brother. David, of course, wanted, *demanded*, that I not neglect him just because of my brother's unfortunate condition. We argued. Boy, did we argue! I'd never stood up to him before. . . ." Mandy sighed again, then leveled her gaze at Luke to gauge his reaction. "How am I doing at true confessions?"

"Splendid," he replied somberly. He looked uncomfortable.

"Yeah, splendid," she repeated, sipping her hot beverage.

"Hey, lady." He reached across the table and, with whisper softness, touched his hand to her short hair. "You make a delicious cup of cocoa."

"Keep it light, huh?" she observed.

"I offered to listen." His emotion-filled eyes held her gaze. "I'm listening."

"Well, that's most of it in a nutshell. Ben's illness and his subsequent death were the beginning of the end of my marriage. I know it would never have survived a lifetime. Marriage ought to be a partnership, not a monarchy."

"How long did it survive?"

"Four very long years. But the marriage was over before that." She hesitated. "I was so blind I didn't see the end coming."

"Were you working?"

"Part-time. David wanted a dutiful little hausfrau. I played the part for him, but not to his liking. He resented the time my job took away from *his* house."

"You weren't out on your own then, were you?" Luke asked.

"No. Burke and Benson began about two years ago. After my divorce."

"And now it's everything to you?"

Mandy raised the steaming mug of cocoa to her lips and took a quick sip. "Everything," she stressed, nodding. "You've got that right."

"Family. Husband. Lover. Child . . ." he muttered staring at her mouth.

"Oh, no," she teased, snaking her tongue out to lick a trace of sweetness from her upper lip. "I've found another lover."

"Yeah?" He grinned his pleasure.

"Yeah," she replied.

Luke placed his mug on the tabletop with a solid thud, then reached across the table again, taking Mandy's small hand in his.

"Show me," he dared softly.

_____ THREE _____

The following Saturday morning, instead of leaving at dawn as he had for weeks, Luke stayed in bed with Mandy, plying her with seductive kisses and, eventually, making slow, sweet love to her.

He felt comfortable in her bed, and comfortable with her. Since there was nowhere else he had to be, he lingered, knowing he was setting a precedent and hoping he wasn't overstepping the boundaries of their no-strings agreement. He suspected Mandy wouldn't object. He'd sensed a closeness evolving from their intimacy and their heart-to-heart talks.

Drawing her into a loose embrace, he asked, "What's a guy have to do around here to get invited to breakfast?"

"First you want my body, now my food?" she teased, playfully tweaking his mustache.

"Only if you're willing." He captured her slender fingers and pressed them to his lips.

"And what are you planning to do while I'm slaving in the kitchen? Do you think I'm going to let you sleep while I work?"

"Yeah, well . . ." He planted moist kisses on her palm. "I was thinking more along the lines of a shower," he explained, feeling marginally hesitant about inviting himself for breakfast *and* a shower. "Feel free to join me if you'd like."

"I'd like!" Her eyes conveyed her obvious delight. "But that still doesn't explain what you're gonna do while I cook."

"Okay, okay," he conceded. "I'll help."

"You mean you can cook?"

"I manage not to make a total fool of myself in the kitchen."

"Somehow I can't picture you making a fool of yourself in any situation," Mandy said.

"Ah, my facade remains intact."

"I didn't say that, MacLaren," she informed him, poking at his chest with her index finger. "You're more transparent than you think, that's all."

"Say, *Dr*. Burke, can we continue this analysis after our shower, say, over breakfast? I'm hungry." He pulled her to the side of the bed with him.

"You know, MacLaren," she began as they made their way toward the bathroom amid much tickling and poking and prodding, "You don't give as much as you get."

"No, lady?" he growled, grabbing her and pinning her against the cold tile wall of the bathroom. "You want me to give you more?" He pressed his long, lean, fully aroused body against hers. "You want me to give to you in the shower, Mandy? Or on the floor?"

He smothered her reply with hard, probing kisses. Then, in one surprising movement, he lowered them to the bathroom carpet, allowing her no chance whatsoever to reply. His mouth never left hers. His busy hands slid over her silky flesh, arousing her, taking and teasing her budding nipples until she arched instinctively toward him.

Still he prolonged his passionate foreplay. Mandy writhed and pressed her body urgently against his, silently begging him to join her. But he did not. One large hand inched provocatively along her heated flesh, touching and caressing her heaving rib cage, her small waist, the gentle curve of her hipbone, at last reaching the warm moistness that was more than proof of her readiness for him. As his fingers tantalized, she moaned beneath him.

"You wanted me to give, lady," he murmured. "I'll give you so much, you'll never forget," he told her, grabbing her hips as he thrust inside her, at last beginning their union.

"Better?" he breathed. "Am I giving enough?"

"More," she murmured.

"More," he echoed, thrusting deeply into her. "Everything, sweet angel. All I have."

Breakfast became brunch. After the loving, after the shower. They worked side by side in the kitchen, broiling thick slices of Canadian bacon, frying potatoes, and preparing a citrus salad with oranges and grapefruit. While Luke made coffee, Mandy set the table for a cozy brunch. She even found a candle.

"Ready?" Luke inquired, as he watched her carry the lighted candle toward him. The table looked as if it had been prepared for a magazine photograph, not for a lovers' brunch. And Mandy, standing over the flickering flame, was perfection wrapped in a midnight-blue negligee that had more slits than fabric. Her face was flushed with warmth in the aftermath of the shower and their loving, and her aquamarine eyes danced mischievously as she glanced at him.

"Ready," she responded, smiling as she sat down.

"We should do this more often," he suggested.

"The bathroom floor, the shower, or breakfast?" she queried in a nonchalant voice.

Smiling his most devastating smile, he replied, "All three. And this is brunch."

"Where'd you learn to broil Canadian bacon to such perfection?" Mandy wondered out loud.

Luke stabbed a large piece of potato. "Brianna."

"Who's Brianna?" she queried. "Or shouldn't I ask?"

"My brother's wife. She thinks I should be able to feed my nephew more than cold cereal. Every now and then she coerces me into "helping" her cook. In reality, she tells me exactly what has to be done, then stands back and watches. Great little lady," he added, reaching for his coffee cup.

"I meant what I said earlier," Mandy told him, changing the subject abruptly. "You don't give much, Luke."

His fork thunked heavily onto the tabletop. He glared at her. "I thought I'd taken care of that little matter," he said, studying her solemnly. "You weren't satisfied?"

Mandy lowered her eyelids. "You know very well I was satisfied." She took a deep breath, held it for a minute, then slowly released it.

"Physically, we're a perfect match. No one could be better. . . . But, I don't really know you, Luke. You listen to me and I appreciate that. I *need* that. But you've got to be able to give up some of yourself."

"Why?"

"Why?" she repeated dumbly. "I don't know. Just because. You want more potatoes?"

"Please," he replied. He studied her as she rose gracefully and crossed the room to get his food. He wasn't quite sure what she wanted from him, but from the vague look of annoyance he saw on her face, he knew she expected something.

"Coffee?" she asked, lifting the carafe with her free hand.

He nodded. His gaze followed her as she returned to the table and refreshed his drink. "What is it you want from me?" he queried. "That is, over and above the physical relationship that we both agree is most gratifying."

"I'm not sure. I guess I'd like you to share more of yourself. For instance, tell me more about your family." She pushed a section of grapefruit around in her dish. "I feel as if I've practically bared my soul to you on several occasions. I guess I have the impression you don't feel comfortable enough with me to do the same."

She raised her eyes to meet his direct gaze. Shrugging her shoulders, she explained, "I'd like you to know I'm just as capable as you are of being a good listener."

"I don't doubt that. If you'll remember, I've already dumped my sorrows in your lap." He held up his hand to stop whatever it was she had opened her mouth to say. "The less said about that, lady, the better I'll feel. Now, you want to know something abut the MacLaren clan, do you?"

"If you're willing." She nodded her agreement. "I felt silly a few minutes ago when I had to ask who Brianna was."

"Brianna Dugan MacLaren is five tiny feet of beautiful woman. She and my oldest brother, Jess, are very happily married. They have two kids, a dog, a cat, and a huge Victorian house several blocks from my parents'. My parents, by the way, have been blissfully married for more than thirty years. Dad owns and operates MacLaren Shipbuilders, the shipbuilding establishment passed on to him by his father and grandfather. Mom thrives on home, kids, and noise.''

Mandy savored a bite of tangy grapefruit, then licked the juice from her lips. ''Does your brother work for your father?''

''No, he doesn't,'' Luke replied. ''He followed in the footsteps of an errant uncle who turned his back on the family business to become a lawyer. My uncle, his son, and my brother have a thriving law practice, Family Law.''

Mandy's quiet ''ohhh'' lasted a few meaningful seconds longer than necessary.

''You've heard of Family Law?''

''I've, um, had firsthand experience with your . . . cousin, I guess. James MacLaren?''

''Cousin. Right.''

Mandy splashed coffee onto the table as she poured herself another cup.

''What's wrong?'' Luke asked, concern evident as he studied the fine lines of tension in her face.

''I'm, um, uncomfortable with that little bit of information, if you must know.''

''There's no reason for you to be,'' he said.

''Probably not,'' she agreed. ''My divorce was kind of nasty.''

''They are professionals,'' he reminded her. ''Shall we discuss something safe? Less personal?''

''No. Go on. Tell me about the next brother,'' she prompted.

''That would be Andrew. Drew. He's one of a kind. A pilot. Right now he's flying for an organization that provides famine relief. Says those poor starving kids shouldn't have to suffer because of a government that isn't well managed. He's right, knows he is, and tries to fight the system as best as possible.

''My sister Sara has been happily married to her high

school sweetheart for five years. They have a little daughter who is an exact replica of my sister, and a new baby girl. Ted's a pharmaceutical representative and one of my closet friends.

"Rachel is twenty-two, a biology major in college. She says she's giving considerable thought to becoming a doctor. We all told her to go for it, but I doubt she will.

"And then comes Ethan. The rogue. Even my dad says he's probably the reincarnation of some long-forgotten rascal forefather. He's a charmer. Always has been. Never fails to get exactly what he wants. Sara says it's his smile. She says it's heart-stopping. Added to that, the kid's always been an incurable flirt. He's had more girlfriends than the rest of us combined. The kid has no staying power. We love him in spite of himself."

He smiled at Mandy and, on impulse, winked. "We love him unconditionally, because he's ours," he added.

"I envy you," she stated, her voice quiet. "The way you look when you speak of your family . . . warm and loving. Makes me more aware of what I've missed."

"Yeah," he mumbled. "Sorry, Mandy. I didn't mean—"

"No," she interrupted, "I wanted to know about them. You don't have to apologize. But, you know, MacLaren, if you feel that bad . . . you could volunteer to wash the breakfast dishes."

"Actually, my dear, I would prefer washing you."

"I'm clean," she reminded him. "We showered. Or did you forget?"

"No way!" he laughed. "I was merely explaining my preference."

"And what about the dishes?"

"I suppose I could offer to help," he conceded. "It'll cost you, though."

"Cost me?" Her brows furrowed as she pondered his remark.

"Yeah." He nodded several times.

"What's your . . . fee?" she asked.

"I think I'd like a massage. Parts of me may need extra special attention after all that physical activity earlier."

Mandy laughed. "You are insatiable and, I suspect, every bit as incorrigible as your brother Ethan. You want more of the same, huh?"

"The same? No," he quipped innocently. "We can vary place, position, technique."

"Luke!" she gasped.

"You're satisfied with the technique, are you? Okay, I won't alter that."

She laughed harder, shaking her head in amazement. "I've been sleeping with a crazy person," she said.

"Sleeping?" Luke's eyebrows raised. "You've been sleeping while I've been working my buns off trying to satisfy you?"

"Must have been worth the effort," Mandy said. "You've got great buns."

"Yeah, well, all that sleeping must be good for you, too, lady. You're looking better all the time."

"Thanks," she said. "I think." She placed her hand over his just as he reached for his coffee mug. "Explain what *better* means."

"More beautiful. More gorgeous, if that's possible. More relaxed, less harried, and much more feminine than I imagined possible when I first met you," he stated candidly. "That naughty little negligee you're wearing is a definite improvement over the austere business suit you wore way back when."

"I wear the suit to work, Luke. You aren't suggesting I sell houses dressed like this, are you?"

He laughed again, a low rumbling laugh that came from deep within him.

"You might sell beds dressed like that. Perhaps your overall sales would increase, but you'd jeopardize your reputation and get propositioned by a great number of clients, married and otherwise. Does your business mean that much to you?"

"Definitely not!" she emphasized. "And just to clarify one other little matter, no one else has been privileged to see me as undressed as you have."

"Mandy," his stern voice immediately drew her attention, "that matter didn't need any clarification. We've been over this. This is a very unique, very private relationship. I'll admit to having a number of women before Maggie, but I've never before been this physically involved with anyone."

"Guess I get a little defensive," she acknowledged.

"No need."

"Right."

"Dishes first? Or should we succumb to the desires of the flesh?"

"You're gonna hate my answer," she informed him, making a face at him as she spoke.

He grinned. "Which is?"

"Dishes first. I ate so much I'm afraid that *massage* you wanted wouldn't quite measure up to your high expectations."

"Okay, dishes first," he agreed amicably. "See how pleasant I can be when I know I'm not being denied, only postponed?"

"Incorrigible," she muttered.

"Don't forget insatiable."

"Cute, MacLaren."

"And cute?" he asked. "I'd rather be considered

devastating or handsome than cute. But for now, I'll just accept whatever small compliments I can garner—''

"Luke," she interrupted, "bring your *cute* buns over here and dry these dishes!''

Mandy finished work early on Friday. The house she'd planned to show to an elderly couple that afternoon had been taken off the market in the morning. Instead of scheduling another prospect, she went home.

The apartment was too quiet. She flipped the radio to an easy-listening station to have a comforting noise in the background.

She stripped her steel-gray work suit and burgundy blouse from her body, removed her slip and ultrafeminine underwear, dusted herself with a fragrant powder, and slid into a green paisley caftan. The luxurious fabric felt cool against her skin.

Back in the living room she curled up in a corner of the couch, opened the lamp-table drawer, and pulled out her quilting square. This was her way of relaxing, even though she didn't often have the time. She had completed a quilt months ago, but this one seemed to be taking forever. Mandy figured she had finished no more than one third of it. There was no better time than the present to make some progress. In all likelihood it would be hours before Luke arrived.

Weeks ago she had realized that he rarely made an appearance before eleven on Friday nights. She had never asked why. She accepted it as part of their no-strings relationship.

As she pushed the needle through the fabric, she smiled to herself. She liked Luke. She was comfortable with him. Granted, they had an odd sort of arrangement, but it suited their needs. At least for the time being.

Mandy was glad she was able to meet his needs. She

had failed miserably at meeting David's—fallen way short of the mark. Oh, she had tried, really tried, to please him, to be all he had expected, all he had demanded. But in the end, when it came down to the wire, she hadn't measured up. And David had bluntly told her she wasn't enough woman for him.

For a long time after that she hadn't felt much like a woman, either. She'd felt like a failure. A reject nobody wanted. But she had eventually clawed her way inch by inch out of the abyss that was once her life. She had jumped at the chance to start her own business, determined to be successful at something.

Now, business was her driving force, her reason for eating, sleeping, waking, breathing. Her hard-hitting plan of attack had, at long last, brought her a certain amount of success in her field.

When she wanted company, she had a few close friends. Occasionally she had dated—very occasionally. But she had made a point never to get involved. There was no way she would set herself up for that kind of hurt again.

And then Luke MacLaren had sauntered into her life and her bed. He'd smiled that devastating smile, appraised her with those sad green eyes, and she'd agreed to this peculiar relationship.

She acknowledged that, for her part, it wasn't merely physical anymore. She cared about him. She couldn't quite fathom why such a likable guy with such a solid background would latch on to her. But whatever the reason, she was grateful. She accepted the fact that sooner or later the key she had given him would not turn in the lock as often, sooner or later he wouldn't stop by at all. She knew very well when his hurt had healed, when his feeling of rejection had passed, he would want a real relationship with a woman. Then she would have to advise him to find someone else. But for now, Mandy was grateful. For now, she was content to be wrapped in Luke's arms at night, blissfully satisfied. . . .

He woke her with a soft, tantalizing kiss. Her eyes fluttered open slowly, focusing on the lips so close to her own.

"Hi, lady," he whispered, brushing his warm mouth against hers. "Want to go to bed with me?"

"Not tonight," she murmured, her husky voice whisper-soft. "I have other plans."

"The couch or the floor?" he asked, shrugging out of his shirt.

"You're still dressed!" She hadn't realized he was fully clothed until that moment.

"Yeah, got as far as my zipper and I couldn't wait to taste your lips," he said, smothering her mouth in the same breath.

"Mmmm. The couch," Mandy murmured.

"Just a sec."

"Slow tonight, aren't you, old man?" she taunted.

"Slight delay," he admitted sheepishly. "Misplaced this helpful little number." He held up one of the small foil packages that he was never without.

Mandy smiled. *Incorrigible*, she thought to herself. *Open, honest* . . . Her eyes feasted on him as he hurried to remove the remainder of his clothes. *Sexy. Aroused.*

"I thought you had your pockets full of those little packages," she teased.

He gathered her into his arms. "I empty my pockets into your night-table drawer frequently, in case you haven't noticed. My supply is in the other room."

"Too lazy to carry me in there?" she challenged.

He pinned her to the couch. "This was your choice, lady. And this is where we're gonna do it!"

"You talk too much, MacLaren," she scolded.

He pressed his lips to hers and not another word was exchanged until much later.

"Luke? It's Saturday, isn't it?" she whispered in the dark. "Are you leaving?"

"Yeah. I promised Noah I'd take him fishing."

"Who's Noah?"

"My nephew."

"It's still dark. You're getting out of bed at this ungodly hour to go fishing?"

"Yeah," he said. "You don't sound like you believe me."

"I . . . don't," she admitted.

"Well, I am," he asserted.

"Fine."

"Mandy, what's the problem here?"

"The problem is that it's four A.M. and you're leaving. I expected you to stay. You've been here for breakfast the last few Saturdays—"

"Today I'm going fishing," he declared calmly. "I should have told you last night. My mistake. It's no big deal, Mandy. I promised Noah we'd go fishing."

"So go," she snapped.

"Like that, is it, lady?" He took two steps to the bed and was on top of her. "I have time for a quickie," he whispered.

Mandy gave no thought to protest. She was aroused and willing before he hit the bed. As soon as his lean body pressed her to the mattress, as soon as his lips captured hers, she responded wholeheartedly to his every command, both spoken and unspoken.

His quickie became a long, leisurely loving. And to her surprise, he didn't pull away but lingered afterward, holding her close and kissing her senseless.

At five o'clock, he murmured in her ear, "I'm late.

How am I gonna explain to a six-year-old that I stopped for a quickie and lost track of time?''

"Why don't you tell him your alarm didn't go off."

"You're suggesting I lie to my nephew? Big brother will have my hide."

"Do you think big brother wants you to tell his son you were in bed with a wanton woman?"

"Big brother is very big on truth."

"Sure," she said. "Try the honest approach. 'Listen, Noah, I was late 'cause I was having sex.' "

Luke's body shook with amusement. "You've made your point, lady. I'll lie."

"Which one is big brother? I've forgotten his name."

"Jess." He kissed her on the nose. "I gotta go now."

"Noah must be really special." The words were out before she realized she'd spoken.

Luke's eyes were gentle as he studied her. "Are you jealous of a six-year-old?"

"No!" she denied quickly. Then realizing she couldn't lie to him, she added, "Well, maybe . . ."

"Okay. I'm already late. I'll tell my brother the truth. He ought to understand. Now, listen up. Noah *is* special. Remember I told you my brother had an automobile accident?"

"I remember. You said he was almost killed."

"Right," he acknowledged. "Well, Noah was conceived before the accident, before Jess and Brianna were married. It's a long story, so I'm gonna shorten it for right now. Jess had a severe head injury that left him with amnesia. He couldn't remember the year prior to the accident. Unfortunately he had no memory of Brianna. Five years after the accident, they became reacquainted, and shortly after that they were married. Noah was cheated out of a dad for a few years, and, well, I got close to him before Jess did. I've maintained the relationship. It means a lot to me. It's helpful to Jess and Brianna, too. Gives them the time together that they need.'' He paused, his gaze fastened on her. ''Now do you understand why I'm leaving this warm bed and your delightful body?''

Mandy nodded. ''For your family,'' she said quietly. ''You're going to make a terrific father someday, Luke.''

''Don't I wish!'' he bit out. ''But for now I'll have to settle for being a terrific uncle.'' He planted a warm, probing kiss on her inviting lips. ''I gotta leave,'' he whispered.

Five minutes later he was dressed and gone.

FOUR

"You're late," Jess accused, scowling as Luke stepped through the doorway and entered the spacious kitchen.

"Uncle Luke, you're here! Oh, boy! Can we leave now?"

"Hi, sport," Luke grinned at Noah and swept the child into his arms. "Sorry I'm late. My alarm didn't go off. Give me a few minutes to talk with your dad and I'll be ready to go."

"Okay," the little boy agreed. "But only a couple minutes, Uncle Luke. The fish can't wait much longer."

"Deal," Luke replied. He released the child and turned to face the disapproving stare of his older brother. "Sorry. I know he's disappointed. I am awfully late."

"Almost two hours. What happened? Did you forget to set your alarm?"

"No. I lied to Noah."

Jess's scowl deepened. "I assume you have a good reason?"

"You wouldn't have wanted me to tell him the truth."

"And why not? You know we're always honest with Noah. We don't keep things from him. Why should this morning be any different?"

"You want the truth, right?"

"Right."

Luke grinned. "Truth is, the lady didn't believe I was crawling out of her bed to go fishing with a six-year-old."

A faint smile began to grow on Jess's face. "Took some convincing?" he inquired.

"I didn't want her to doubt my word," Luke explained.

"And did she?"

"Initially, but I convinced her otherwise."

"That's better than getting drunk—or trashing the tower room," Jess remarked matter-of-factly. "Let's go fishing. Noah won't wait much longer."

"You're coming along?"

"I've been up with Noah for two hours waiting for you. I may as well."

"Where's Brianna?"

"She's upstairs writing."

"If it makes any difference, I am sorry," Luke offered.

"Forget it," Jess told him. "I understand your diversion. Let's go."

The morning was beautiful. The air was crisp and cool, the waters calm. Gentle spring breezes swirled all around. The three fishermen were highly successful. Noah was the center of attention and loved it. He had the distinction of catching the most fish and, consequently, was quite puffed up with pride. Jess and Luke devoted their time to encouraging and helping the child and tried in vain to do some serious fishing themselves.

Instead, Luke found himself thinking about his early-morning encounter with Mandy. He remembered the tone of her voice, the hint of hurt and jealousy she had tried to hide. She'd expected him to stay for breakfast, and if he hadn't had other plans, he would have.

She had been right. Saturday breakfast had become part of their routine. She shouldn't have assumed as much, but wasn't he making the same assumption simply by hanging around on Saturday mornings?

He wasn't angry or annoyed with her. After all, he had been behaving in a similar manner. They were good together. He enjoyed her company, even craved it sometimes. She hadn't made demands. She hadn't asked him for anything or expected more than a physical relationship. He liked their arrangement. He was comfortable with it. So comfortable, in fact, he wasn't sure how long it had been since he'd slept in his own bed.

Nor did he care how long it had been. The pain of losing Maggie was receding. It didn't hurt quite so much anymore to think about her, especially when he could lose himself in Mandy's bed. It was painful remembering how Maggie had shattered his dreams. He wanted a wife and family desperately.

Sometimes he wondered how he'd handle seeing her again. She and Sara were such good friends, running into her was inevitable. He wasn't sure he could pretend friendship with the woman who had rejected the idea of marriage to him.

Time. It always came back to that. Time was what he needed most. Distance from past emotional involvement. Why couldn't emotional wounds heal as quickly as flesh wounds? Maggie had turned off her affection.

Why couldn't he? He would probably be fool enough to take her back and let her walk all over him again.

No! He wouldn't be that kind of jerk a second time. No woman was ever going to use him, then discard him like yesterday's news. He would never give another woman the chance to get that close. It just wasn't worth the agony afterward.

This relationship with Mandy was the best thing going. Sex, good sex, whenever he needed it. And, best of all, no strings, no commitments. He was free to come and go as he chose. He'd found a solution and he was going to forget all his past misery and enjoy his current freedom, his newfound lifestyle, and his new lady. . . .

His new lady? He wondered where that thought had come from. In a way he supposed she was his lady. Their agreement had evolved into a relationship. This morning's incident was all the proof he needed that invisible strings linked them.

He had heard disbelief and hurt in her voice. But more than that, he'd sensed it on some level, then read it in her eyes. He'd responded to her without hesitation. And, he silently admitted, without regret. Mandy's warmth and friendship were reason enough not to question the strength of those invisible strings.

After dinner with Jess and Brianna, Luke drove to his parents' home. As usual, the big old house was filled with laughter and noise. Ethan had invited a few friends, who had brought their dates, and when Luke walked in the kitchen, he found the counters lined with pizzas.

His parents had taken refuge in the den. His mother was working on a quilting square. His father was reading a book. Luke realized the elder MacLarens had Chopin playing on the stereo. He heard the quiet strains of piano music when Ethan changed tapes in the other room.

Luke challenged his father to a game of chess and the two of them played for hours. Shortly before midnight, Jonas won the game. Luke grinned, acknowledging that sooner or later one of them had to emerge victorious. He said good night to his parents, went through the kitchen, grabbed a slice of cold pizza, then made his way to the back of the house and up to his room.

He needed a shower and a change of clothes. That was his first order of business. Yet after a lengthy shower, he moved restlessly around the apartment. He wanted to go to Mandy, but considering the hour, he hesitated.

The uneasiness lingered. It had been weeks since he'd slept alone, and he didn't want to be alone tonight. Even if he could shake the nagging edginess and relax, there was no way he could sleep. The kids downstairs were still going strong.

His decision made, Luke stuffed his wallet into his back pocket, grabbed his jacket, and clutching his key case in his fist, strode outside to the car.

Twenty minutes later, he unlocked Mandy's apartment door, juggling boxes of doughnuts and danish and a grocery bag containing fresh oranges and a carton of milk.

He entered the apartment quietly, not wanting to frighten her out of a deep sleep. He took the packages into the kitchen and began to put things away, being careful not to awaken Mandy.

He placed the milk and oranges in the refrigerator, left the doughnuts and pastries on the counter, and began to prepare the coffee pot for the next morning. That was the least he could do after coming in at this late hour.

As he turned toward the sink to fill the pot with water, he spied Mandy. She was standing near the doorway, watching him.

She looked enticing, her face flushed with drowsiness, her eyelids still heavy from sleep. She wore a short, lavender negligee with a plunging neckline that left very little to the imagination. His stomach knotted with desire.

"Hi. Hope I didn't wake you. Thought I'd get breakfast ready before I came to bed."

"Something woke me," she explained quietly. "Probably the squeaky refrigerator door."

"Sorry," he offered.

"I'm glad you're here, Luke," Mandy said, trying to disguise the relief she felt at the sight of him. She had decided it was too late to expect him, and she had, after all, caused the delay that morning.

"I didn't want to sleep alone," he admitted.

"Neither did I."

"You want to talk about what happened this morning?" he asked.

"Do you want me to apologize for making you late?" she countered.

"No, Mandy. I wasn't late because of you. I was nearly dressed and ready to leave. We both know I could have left without an explanation. Neither of us would have been satisfied with that outcome."

"Did you feel obligated to offer me that explanation?"

"To some extent, yes. I owe you that much."

"We said no strings," she reminded him.

"Yeah, right. No strings," he repeated. But the words tasted odd as he spoke them, and somewhere in his mind a niggling protest begged to be heard. "However, Amanda Burke, you expected me to stay for breakfast. . . . And the truth is, I would have, had it not been for my previous plans. I assumed the same as you.''

"No big deal. You explained. I understand." She shrugged her shoulders.

"My family comes first—"

"I know," she interrupted.

"There will be more occasions like this."

"Okay. I realize that."

"I'm sorry I neglected to mention the fishing expedition."

"Luke," she said, her voice rising in mild agitation, "you certainly don't need to apologize. No strings. You don't owe me an explanation."

"You were upset," he pointed out.

Mandy looked at him standing there, leaning casually against the sink. Concern was written all over his face.

"I admit I was upset," she finally revealed. "I'm unaccustomed to having you disappear so early and so hastily from my bed. It took me by surprise . . . confused me."

"You didn't want to discuss those feelings with me, did you?"

She sighed, her breath escaping little by little. "No," she admitted ruefully.

"I thought we were always honest with each other."

"Yeah. Okay. We usually are. My mistake," she conceded.

"Let's get our act together, lady," he ordered lightheartedly. "No more mistakes. If you think I'm being an inconsiderate bastard, tell me. Deal?"

She bobbed her head in agreement. "It's a deal."

"How about we shake on it?" he teased, reaching one lanky arm in her direction.

"Shake?"

"Yeah, well," he replied, his grin widening. "First

we shake, and then—" he smiled broadly "—we get to the good stuff."

"Promises, promises," she taunted. "You're still dressed."

"Yeah," he observed, looking down at his jean-clad legs, then slowly raising his eyes to fasten on her sleepy figure.

"Undress me, Mandy," he commanded quietly.

Luke not only stayed for breakfast, but the entire morning as well. They put the time to good use, leisurely exploring each other's bodies, memorizing every intimate inch. They showered together and made love slowly, savoring every sensual moment.

When Luke's stomach rumbled rudely beneath Mandy's ear as she lay curled against him, she reached around and tickled his ribs.

"You should have told me you were hungry again!" she scolded.

"Didn't want to wear out my welcome, begging two meals from you in one day," he returned.

"I can see where that might seem rather presumptuous of you," she agreed, her eyes dancing with delight as she traced his mustache with her finger.

"Wanna get dressed and go out for a burger?" he asked.

"I'd rather eat right here. We could have an intimate, elegant lunch in bed. I think I've got a small casserole of chicken divan in the freezer. I'll just pop it in the microwave and assemble a green salad. What do you think?"

"Sounds delicious . . ." He hesitated.

"But you don't like that idea, do you?" she guessed.

"I just wanted something quick, not a meal. Sunday evening, Mom always has everyone for dinner."

"Oh," she remarked, feeling strangely left out.

Luke sensed her alienation, just as he had Saturday morning. "Oh, yourself," he came back at her. Then he twisted, changing position to lie on top of her. As he kissed her, he made a conscious effort to show Mandy that he was there with her, that she wasn't alone or in any way separate.

When he felt her relax again, he growled against her mouth, "Lady, you made me an offer I can't refuse. Lunch in bed with you sounds inviting . . . exciting. . . ." He watched the expressions playing across her face. "Kinky." She smiled. "I'll feed you. You'll feed me." She raised her eyebrows in mock astonishment. "Who knows where the pleasure will end," he commented suggestively.

"I do," she supplied. "You'll get dressed and go home for dinner."

"Yeah," he muttered as a smidgen of guilt made its presence known, "but I'll come back here for my dessert. . . ." He covered her mouth hungrily, tasting the delights she offered.

Mandy buried her fingers in his thick hair and held him close. When he moved to break away, she silently encouraged him to prolong the embrace. He nibbled at her lips. She parted them, inviting him to relish the sweetness of her mouth. She gave. He took. Slowly, ever so slowly, the kiss drew to an end.

"Chocolate cake?" she murmured.

"What?"

"For dessert. Do you want chocolate cake for dessert?"

"No," he growled. "I want more of what I just had."

"No cake?"

"Not necessary."

"But if I made it?"

"I have an enormous appetite. You could probably

convince me to indulge, say about midnight, after I've sampled—make that feasted on—the dessert I intend to have.''

"You have a thing for midnight snacks, you know, MacLaren.''

"Must be the company I keep," he quipped. "All the *physical activity* makes me hungry at odd hours. And speaking of quirks, lady, you have a *thing* for chocolate, don't you?''

"Oh, no! True confessions again? You've discovered my Achilles' heel," she giggled. "I can be bought with chocolate. It's my one great passion. Drat! I was hoping you wouldn't suspect. Now you've got something to hold over my head.''

"Right," he confirmed, stroking his mustache in true villain fashion. "Now I'll be able to have my way with you more often. All I have to do is ply you with chocolate. Easy. E-A-S-Y!''

"As if I wasn't easy enough," she muttered.

Luke laughed, a deep, rich laugh. "Lady, you're a pushover. I wouldn't want you any other way." He gave her derriere a tender but playful squeeze. "Do you intend to heat the casserole, or merely warm my buns?''

"Luke MacLaren!" she scolded. "You are—''

"I know," he interrupted, "incorrigible! And hungry, Mandy. I'm hungry!''

"Okay, message received. The food will be ready in no time," she said, quickly twisting away from him and out of bed.

"Feed me. Please, feed me," he pleaded in his best starving-man voice.

Mandy laughed merrily at his antics as she hurried from the room to prepare their meal.

He appeared to be asleep when she returned. Juggling the large tray laden with food, she stood in the doorway studying him. His muscular body, naked except for tight black briefs, lay stretched out comfortably on her pink satin sheets. He looked as if he belonged there. The sight of him like that tugged at her heartstrings. He was more than just a friend, more than just a superb lover. Much more, she acknowledged silently.

She had spent a large part of the previous day analyzing her reaction to his early-morning departure. And she had decided she would be satisfied with however much of himself he deigned to share. She would give him the freedom he professed to need. She would be there for him if he chose to share with her. She could handle that. She had agreed to "no strings." And for now, for her own sake, she would try to keep up appearances.

"Luke," she whispered, surprised when his eyes opened immediately and fastened on her. "You're awake!"

"Just resting my eyes," he told her. "Here, let me help you with the tray."

They set up their intimate luncheon, sharing the task without speaking. The unusual silence prevailed as they began to eat. More than half the food was devoured before either of them said a word.

"Delicious," he declared. "You are a superb cook."

"Thanks," she murmured.

"You like to cook, don't you?"

"I enjoy it, when I have the time."

"And when is that? You're a busy lady."

"Weekends," she replied, playing with her salad. "And some evenings, if I'm home early. I prepare enough for several meals and freeze the extra to use when I'm rushed."

Luke's silence served as a magnet. Her aquamarine eyes lifted to meet his, fastened, then held.

"What's wrong?" She was bothered by the intensity of their wordless exchange.

"I'm impressed, that's all," he revealed. "Underneath that cool businesswoman veneer, I believe I detect the heart of a—what was that term you used?—hausfrau?"

"Think you're smart, don't you?" she chided.

"I am," was his quick retort. "And I'm right, aren't I?"

"Maybe," she admitted reluctantly. She stabbed at a tomato with forced enthusiasm.

Luke observed her rigid posture, witnessed her evasive actions, then grinned, knowingly. "Hit a nerve?" he remarked, almost too quietly to be heard.

She laid down her fork, sighing in exasperation.

Before she had the chance to speak, he reached out one strong hand, tenderly lifting her chin. He leaned toward her, cautiously, so as not to dump their dinner onto the bed, and brushed soft, tantalizing kisses across her pouting lips.

"Nothing to be ashamed of, tough lady," he whispered. "Some of my favorite people do homey things like cooking and quilting. I like the feminine side of you. Don't try to deny that part of yourself, Mandy, or hide it. I'd rather be acquainted with the whole woman."

"Would you?" she challenged. "This *whole woman* is not what she seems."

"Yeah, I figured that much," he observed shrewdly. "Old wounds, Mandy?"

She nodded.

"Want to talk about it?"

She sighed again and shook her head. "Not today. Maybe some other time. . . ."

"Keep it light?" he suggested.

"Yeah," she agreed, smiling into his murky eyes.

Mandy was the first to break eye contact. Today it seemed as if Luke were silently reaching for the woman inside, the one she worked so hard to conceal. Each time their eyes met, his unspoken inquiries probed deeper. Right now her emotions were dangerously close to the surface and she wasn't ready to deal with them—or his questions.

"Tell me what's wrong," he coaxed, his voice oozing concern. "I know something is bothering you."

"It's nothing" was her hasty reply.

"Mandy . . ." he began, his tone severe.

"Does your family really get together each week for Sunday dinner?" Changing the subject was a ploy, but asking about his family was brilliant. She was sure it would work.

"Yeah," he answered.

"All of them?" she asked, amazed.

"All of them," he emphasized, "except Drew, of course. Sometimes he's gone for months."

"Your mom cooks for everyone?"

"She used to do all the cooking," he responded freely, "but Brianna changed that much of the routine. She's always insisted on bringing part of the meal. She brings a salad or dessert or freshly baked bread. Since Brianna broke tradition, Sara's been contributing also, even though the entire world knows Sara hates to cook. She usually brings a vegetable dish. Mom has less work and we get more variety. We eat very well."

"Sounds that way."

"Yeah, well." He cleared his throat. "May I have the same dessert now that I've requested for after dinner this evening?"

Mandy's gaze roamed over his long frame, intentionally resting and lingering on the fabric of his briefs. She took her time answering.

"Perhaps," she teased. "If you promise to help with the dishes afterward."

"And if I refuse to help but ply you with chocolate this evening?"

"You scoundrel!" she accused. "I knew you'd use that information to your benefit!"

Luke hauled her into his arms, laughing. "I'll help you with the dishes and bring you chocolate," he promised as his lips brushed her forehead. "How's that suit?"

Mandy saw undisguised desire flare in Luke's eye's as his head bowed toward hers. "All right," she agreed moments before he tasted her mouth.

"Yeah," he murmured. "Chocolate and good sex. All right!"

The next few weeks Mandy managed to control her newly recognized feelings for Luke without much problem. After all, she was the one who slept in his arms each night. Their routine didn't alter as her feelings deepened and grew. Luke still departed early in the morning just as he had before. Weekends he stayed for breakfast and, when it suited him, for lunch. Their friendship strengthened. Their physical relationship remained as mutually satisfying as ever.

Mandy threw herself into her work each day, devoting long hours to her business, while her partner, Amy Benson, seemed to slack off. At night Mandy made sure she was there, ready for Luke. She would shower or soak before he arrived, depending on how late she had worked and how tired she felt. She indulged herself in a shopping spree one Saturday afternoon and purchased several deliciously provocative lingerie items, which she used to delight him. He never failed to react as she had anticipated to these enticing bits of lace.

For all appearances, their no-strings physical relationship was working. Mandy made a concerted effort to keep it light. After all, she was happier than she had ever been. She had all the benefits of a secure, successful, single businesswoman, plus the pleasure of a warm, satisfying man in her bed each night.

Individually she and Luke were self-reliant. They had no arguments over responsibility, who takes out the trash, who pays the bills, and so on. They bantered about whose turn it was to make the coffee or wash the dishes, but in the end, Luke always shared these tasks, often doing more for her than she anticipated.

He brought groceries more and more frequently, surprising her with an unusual variety of goodies. One afternoon she came home to find he had stopped at a Greek carryout. The kitchen counter was laden with samples of moussaka, spinach-and-cheese pies, Greek salad, and baklava. Several times their meals were prepared at elegant restaurants Luke patronized on his way home from work.

All things considered, she could not complain.

The most difficult time of the day, truly the only time she had to herself to think, was when she was soaking. Sometimes then she felt a twinge of regret. Regret that Luke didn't care more for her. Regret that their relationship was so self-contained and private. Regret that he didn't share his family with her. She knew she would enjoy meeting each of them, but doing so implied forging bonds, strings, attachments. And that was not to be. . . . Sometimes Mandy felt regret that there would be no future for them.

Days and nights marched on pleasurably. But what of a future? What would she do when Luke was ready to move on? Mandy didn't want to face that reality. Life was good to her now. Life was treating her well for a change. And beyond the present? She refused to focus on the possibilities.

FIVE

Mandy heard the phone as she shoved the apartment door open. "This is ridiculous," she muttered, kicking it shut behind her. She balanced the grocery bag precariously on one hip and dropped her attaché case onto an overstuffed chair. As she plunked the bag on the kitchen table, she glared at the phone. What she really wanted was a long, hot shower and some peace and quiet. It was bad enough the office phone had rung nonstop all day. She'd hoped she'd left that annoyance behind her.

Mandy grabbed the telephone and said a polite but reluctant hello.

Luke's deep rumble began without so much as a preliminary hi. "I called to . . . to tell you . . . I—I won't be seeing you for a while."

His speech was halting and his voice cracked strangely, filled with an emotion Mandy couldn't identify.

"Okay," she replied, keeping her voice as even as she could. Hurt and confusion swept through her, yet she sensed that all was not well with Luke. "Are you all right? You sound strange."

Silence was her answer.

"Something *is* wrong," she insisted. "What is it, Luke? Tell me, please." She thought he wasn't going to speak, but as she was about to voice her concern, he broke the heavy silence.

"My . . . God!" he rasped.

Mandy held her breath, waiting for him to continue. From the sound of agony in those two words she knew he was struggling for control.

"This morning . . ." he began, faltering, "there was a . . . a sniper—"

"In the city," Mandy finished for him. "Yes. I heard the news." Filled with an undeniable apprehension, she asked, "Did you know one of the victims?"

"Yeah." His voice broke.

Again she waited, sensing the battle of strong emotions gripping him. It seemed like a short eternity before he continued, and when he did, the whispered word was nearly inaudible.

"Ted."

"Ted," she repeated, her mind racing to place the name. The knowledge came swiftly, and with it, an instantaneous knotting of her stomach and a flash of despair weakening her knees. "Sara's husband? Oh, no, Luke . . ." Unexpected tears streamed down her face. She brushed them aside, biting her lip as she sought words of comfort for him.

"I . . . can't . . . talk. . . ." he said. And she knew he'd had to force each word.

Mandy swallowed the lump that seemed to fill her throat. "I'm so sorry, Luke," she murmured. "Please—" But when she realized he had hung up, she stopped midsentence and replaced the receiver.

For several endless, anguished moments she stood with her hand glued to the telephone, her mind replaying their conversation. Then she stumbled toward the couch, allowing the tears to fall freely now that no one would know. She fell back onto the cushions and picked up a plump pillow, hugging it close as she sobbed without restraint.

Luke's family, she thought. *How awful for them!*

She knew what they were feeling. She had been there when Ben had died. And yet, she had known he was dying. She'd had time to prepare. Time to say goodbye and tell him she loved him. That she would always love him. That he was special and she would miss him.

She had watched him die slowly—stayed by his side hour after hour as he wasted away. She had witnessed his agony, his suffering. She had been relieved when, at long last, he was at peace. But always, always she missed him.

It had gotten easier as the days and months and years had passed. But now she wept in despair for Ben, as well as for Luke and Sara and their family.

Knowing Luke was hurting made Mandy even more unhappy. She wanted to be able to talk with him, hold him, and comfort him. She remembered the despair and loneliness she'd felt after Ben's death. She had longed for someone—anyone—to care enough to try to break through her cloak of grief. She wished she could find a way to ease the pain for Luke.

But he had called to tell her not to expect him.

His family was close. They would grieve together and, perhaps, heal together. For a fraction of a second, she envied them their blessing. Then she scolded herself for being so self-pitying and self-centered. The family was grieving and distraught. Thank God they had one another.

And if Luke MacLaren stayed with his family and never made his way back? Well then, she would have to be that much stronger. She would have to add another layer to the facade. A layer that said, ''I don't care. I'm okay, I can handle this alone. I have before. I will again.''

"Darn you, Luke," she muttered. "I want you here with me, not with them. Phooey! We said we'd keep it casual, and look at me, sitting here blubbering like a spoiled child because I can't have what I want." Mandy made a futile attempt to wipe away her tears. "Oh, Luke, I care about you. I care! I don't want you to hurt . . . not like I did. . . .''

It's just not fair, she thought. *Life's not fair. I want to kiss him and make it all better. Or to hold him until the pain is gone. And here I am, and there he is. My hands are tied. I feel useless. Utterly useless. And what good is a silly sobbing female? Absolutely none! He is better off without me. He is better off with his family!*

"If only there were something I could do," she wailed in frustration.

For two days Mandy spent nearly every waking hour absorbed in business. She felt useful, productive. And, best of all, her mind was occupied with thoughts other than Luke and death.

For two nights she slept restlessly, and alone. On the third morning, she picked up the paper while she was drinking a hurried cup of coffee. She was drawn to the news items about the sniper and his capture. When she read the accounts of the bystanders and the plight of the victims' families, she had a different perspective than she'd had before.

These were not just names in a news story. These were real people. Their families were victims, too. Part of each of them had died by the sniper's bullet.

Mandy was overcome with renewed sadness.

Memorial services were being held for Ted O'Roarke the next morning. She pondered paying her respect to

Luke's grieving family. It seemed like the right thing to do. But was it?

She hadn't heard from Luke again. He wouldn't expect her to be at the service. No strings implied no obligations. Except, to her way of thinking, this was different. She'd simply explain that she felt compelled to be there. He ought to understand. She was merely going to sit through the service and pay her respects to the grieving family. Her decision was made.

She slipped unobtrusively into a pew in the back of the large church, then bowed her head in prayer, asking God to comfort the grieving loved ones, to give them guidance in the days to follow. Something about the smell of the old church brought the first wave of memories. The organ music brought the first tears of sadness.

Mandy shifted uncomfortably in the hard, wooden seat and gazed in wondering adoration at the beautiful stained glass windows. This service was going to be much more difficult to endure than she had expected.

Her eyes moved deliberately from one window to the next, not only studying and admiring each, but reflecting on the story depicted there. Next she distracted herself by surveying the intricate design of the front of the church and the array of flowers at the altar.

Inevitably the family group gathered near the casket drew her attention. Ted O'Roarke's loved ones. Luke's family. Mandy's eyes roamed quickly from one to the other, then back again, studying their features, comparing their similarities. It was easy to discern who the MacLaren brothers and sisters were. Five tall, broad-shouldered men—one gray-haired—all with angular, square-jawed faces. All four sons had hints of auburn sunshine in their hair. One of them stood with a petite dark-haired woman. Mandy decided that had to be Jess with Brianna. The older man, their father, was next to an auburn-haired beauty, who Mandy guessed was the widowed Sara. She appeared much too young to be facing this type of crisis.

Mandy swallowed hard, trying to combat tears. Luke had his arm around a slim brunette. His head was bowed toward her, listening as she spoke. They looked as if they belonged together. On top of overwhelming sadness came an acute stab of jealousy. And jealousy was a silly emotion to be experiencing at a memorial service. Mandy scolded herself silently. The woman could be Ted's sister, a cousin, a close family friend, their next-door neighbor. . . .

Whoever she was, she had Luke's complete attention. And Mandy was envious. She wished she were the one standing beside him, speaking softly while he, it appeared, hung on every word.

She looked away, forcing herself to scrutinize the stained glass windows on the opposite side of the church. Jesus ascending into heaven brought the tears welling up, over the brim, down her face.

I miss you, Ben, she thought.

She sat in the sanctuary of the old church, thinking back a few years to the days following Ben's death. The devastating sorrow she had experienced then threatened to close in around her. As she fought against rising despair, she realized the minister had begun to speak.

The service was beautiful, moving, promising them all peace in the hereafter. The eulogy delivered by Mr. MacLaren was quite eloquent. Mandy felt as if she had known Ted personally after hearing the family who loved him so dearly speak of the full life he had lived.

She allowed the tears to flow freely during the service, knowing firsthand it did no good to keep them in check. Grieving was a normal process that should be allowed to follow its course. Healing began sooner when one accepted grief.

As the assembly of relatives and friends of Ted O'Roarke rose for the final hymn, Mandy reached for a handkerchief and attempted to dry her tears. When the last refrain began, she slipped quietly from her place in the back of the church and departed.

She drove home wrapped in a familiar numbness. It was an unwelcome feeling, one she cared not to experience again. Nevertheless it remained in control of her emotions for the duration of the day. She couldn't even force herself to work. Reminders of Ben were everywhere she turned. She finally succumbed and pulled out her photo albums, poring over pictures of the two of them together, enjoying the few pleasures they had shared in his last years. David had been involved with them, for the most part, standing alongside observing, not really belonging to the close unit they were.

Thoughts of David and their disastrous marriage superimposed themselves on memories of Ben, and for a short while Mandy dwelled on the time they had had together. She had tried to be a good wife and, in her own way, had loved David in spite of his ego and his selfishness. When Ben had died and she'd needed David, he'd been little comfort. And in the end, when her world and her dreams came crashing down around her, David had turned his back, walking out of her life, abandoning her when she needed him the most.

The agony, the void she had lived through then was equaled only by the loss of Ben. Remembering, Mandy gave in to her battered emotions and sobbed without restraint.

Eventually she slept, half sitting, half lying on the couch, the photo album forgotten in her lap. . . .

The big house stood, as it had for many years, beneath the shade of the large pine trees. Inside, the family had gathered, but this time it was mutual sadness

that brought them together, not the good-natured camaraderie they usually shared.

Today the house was filled with the love and closeness it had always harbored, and yet the tenor was
different. Instead of the normal laughter, the sounds
inside the house were muted; voices speaking quietly
to one another, consoling, comforting, sharing a rare
moment of sadness.

Alone in his room, Luke sat on the edge of the bed,
his head in his hands, trying not to think or feel, yet
unable to check the flow of his thoughts. Ted was gone.
He would never see his friend again. They had buried
him that morning. Now he lay in darkness for all
eternity.

How could a loving God deny a man the reward of
seeing his daughters grow? How could God deny those
sweet children their father? And why? Why did life
have to be so cruel to innocent children?

And Sara . . . Now Sara would be all alone, never
hearing her husband's voice or sharing his laughter,
never seeing his smile or feeling his touch again. None
of this was fair!

Sara had done nothing to deserve this, and neither
had her daughters. For that matter, neither had he.

Life hadn't treated him kindly of late. He liked the
way it used to be. Sara and Ted and Maggie and Luke
laughing together, playing together. They had been a
foursome since the day Sara introduced her intense
dark-haired friend to her "silly older brother," as she
had dubbed him then.

Luke had been smitten by Maggie from the first. And
Maggie had liked Luke. And ever after it was always
Luke and Maggie—together. They complemented each
other. Sara had been thrilled that her brother and her
best friend were sweethearts, and that her husband and
her brother were such close friends. They'd shared

long-weekend getaways at a cottage on the coast.
They'd rented a sailboat and disappeared together for
ten days one summer. The four of them. Always planning new adventures. Always together.

Maggie dashed off to one place or another to study,
but she returned to relax and play with the group. It
was an established practice. It was as if it had been
ordained or written in stone. Sara and Ted, Maggie and
Luke.

That's how it had been until four months ago when
Maggie had dropped her bombshell, taken wing, and
flown off on her own, leaving him wounded and hurting
in her wake.

The comfortable group that was so much a part of
his life ceased to exist. Sara and Ted had been blessed
with a new baby. Their life had been close to perfect.
His, however, seemed to fall apart. He'd never felt so
alone. Not only alone, but gripped with an emotional
pain he hadn't even known could exist.

And now, like ice water being tossed on a sun-baked
body, he'd discovered the shock of a different kind of
pain. Once before he'd come close to this feeling. But
his brother had survived his physical traumas, and
Luke's emotions had not been this battered.

Maggie, he knew, was alive and well. Tangible but
elusive. If he absolutely *had* to hear her voice, he could
tuck away his pride, pick up the phone, and in a matter
of minutes speak with her. But Ted was gone. He
would never joke with his friend again. And never was
a long, long time. Years would pass without Ted's
friendship. Their foursome had truly crumbled, was
truly destroyed.

Luke liked stability, and the rug had just been yanked
from beneath his feet. A lifetime of happiness, of
dreams, of contentment snuffed out in a matter of
seconds.

"You look like hell," Jess observed, startling Luke from the depths of self-pity.

"That's how I feel," he replied.

"We all do."

Luke looked up. "Who's with Sara?"

"Sara, Brianna, and Rachel are holed up together in Rachel's room. Mom's in the kitchen organizing the mountains of food contributed by caring friends and neighbors."

"That should keep her occupied."

"I suppose it will. Seems to be enough casseroles and cakes to feed this clan for weeks. I heard her mention that the freezer was almost filled to capacity."

"Is anyone actually eating the stuff?"

"I doubt it," Jess returned, sinking into the closest chair. "Shock deadens the appetite. Are you going to be all right, Luke?"

"Don't know," he grumbled. "How're you doing?"

"Brianna and I talked most of the night," Jess revealed soberly. "She's a strong lady . . . a real comfort."

"Yeah, I know."

"Bri believes God places obstacles in our paths, sets up situations such as this, in order that we experience both pain and pleasure. She believes somewhere down the road, Sara will be given great happiness."

"If only I could believe that," Luke muttered in a choked voice.

"Some of us have stronger convictions," Jess said. "Brianna and I have, each in our own way, scraped bottom. I suppose we'll always value what we have now, much more, because of our previous experience."

Luke rose from the bed and studied his brother. "What you two have is rare."

"Rare, special, and very, very beautiful," Jess agreed. "God willing, Sara may find the same."

"God willing," Luke repeated, lifting his eyes heavenward. He walked to the front window and pushed the curtain aside with his index finger. "And where is God today? Sara's world has been destroyed."

"She has two little children to love and care for. A living legacy from her husband."

"Do you think it's fair that they will never know their dad?"

"No, Luke," Jess responded. "It's not fair. Life's not fair. I'll always regret that I missed four years of Noah's life. But I can't change what happened in the past, and neither can Sara."

Luke let the curtain drop and turned to face Jess. "And neither can I?"

"Right."

"So I'm supposed to accept that a benevolent God allowed some crazy to kill my friend?" he asked with a sweeping gesture of his arms.

"I didn't say it wouldn't take time."

"Time," he scoffed. "Hell!"

"This isn't easy for me, either, Luke."

"Yeah, I know. I was already down . . . before I got kicked in the teeth." He leaned back against the deep windowsill, until he was half sitting, half standing.

"You appeared to handle the situation with Maggie smoothly enough this morning," Jess said.

"I guess," Luke responded.

"How does it feel?"

"The changes in my life recently are kind of hard to deal with, you know?"

"You're the one who likes everything to remain the same. Neat little compartments for family and friends.

People paired off two by two. Nothing ever changing. That isn't realistic.''

Luke sighed heavily. "I felt bad when Maggie dumped me, but at least she's alive and well. Ted—'' he closed his eyes ''—Ted is . . . gone.'' He rubbed his hand across his face to erase the images he wanted to forget. "Gone . . . He simply doesn't exist anymore.''

"Sure he does,'' Jess disagreed. "In our memories, in our hearts . . . in his babies' eyes. Ted lives, Luke. Sara won't let go of the vital force that was her husband's life.''

Luke opened tear-filled eyes and stared at his older brother. "How'd you get to be so wise?''

"Wasn't easy, little brother,'' Jess acknowledged. "First I had to fight my way back from death's door. Then I was forced to re-evaluate my purpose in life, and, to make a long story short, I married a terrific lady who shared my grief with me last night.'' Jess slowly filled his lungs with air, then released it in a long, loud sigh. "I suppose you might say I have a different perspective this morning. Brianna's love helps hold me together.''

"Lucky you,'' Luke muttered.

"I knew you'd take Ted's death harder because of your close friendship.'' Jess raked his fingers through his thick auburn hair. "And I know this will sound trite, but damn, Ted wouldn't want you to mope around feeling sorry for yourself! Grieve, Luke. That's fine. But don't dwell on your despair. Get on with your life.''

Luke pursed his lips and gave an acknowledging nod. "I have a . . . friend whose brother died. . . .''

"Then talk to your friend, if talking with me doesn't help. But don't shut yourself away in your room. That's not healthy.''

"Dying isn't healthy, either," Luke returned.

"Unavoidable," Jess muttered.

"Yeah . . ."

"Is this a private discussion or may I join you?" Brianna's soft voice drew both men's attention to the doorway.

"Hi, babe," Jess murmured.

"Brianna." Luke levered himself up from the windowsill and opened his arms to welcome his diminutive sister-in-law.

She needed no further invitation to enter his domain, and moved forward, into his embrace, allowing him to hold her close for moments of sharing and comfort. When she pulled back, she studied Luke's desolate expression, then stood on her tiptoes to place a consoling kiss on his cheek. He returned the gesture automatically.

"Are you going to be all right?" she questioned, gently laying her hand along his jaw.

"Big brother's gonna break my face if I'm not."

She offered him a hesitant smile. "I don't know what's going on, but I'd venture a guess that Jess did not threaten you with bodily harm." Her eyes roamed in silent challenge from one brother to the other. She stepped away from Luke and was immediately enfolded in her husband's strong arms.

"This is the pits," Jess proclaimed. "Each one of us feels lousy. All the hugging in the world doesn't help."

Luke raised one eyebrow. "Jealous?"

"Nope. I understand and respect the deep affection you two maintain for each other."

"Lighten up," Luke begged.

"You're the one who's been dragging his face on the floor," Jess pointed out.

"And you're the one who just finished commenting that we're all feeling down," Brianna reminded him.

"And you have each other," Luke added.

Brianna held up a dainty hand. "Wait just a minute. One of the best things about being part of the MacLaren clan is that no one, I repeat, *no one* need ever be alone. You have one another to lean on. You all have a great capacity for love. Believe me, that is a blessing. And you ought to take full advantage of it."

"End of sermon, Brianna?" Luke asked.

"I didn't mean to preach, only offer a reminder," she defended. "We need our loved ones and our friends right now, much more than we normally would. Jess and I have decided to stay with the family for a few days."

"Until the magic hour when the grieving family decides it's time to return to normalcy," Luke intoned sarcastically.

"Luke!" Jess snapped. "It's important for us to be on hand whenever Sara needs us."

"Yeah, all right. I'm sorry," he apologized. "Basically a sound decision on your part, folks. Sara's going to need us. . . ."

"She's doing very well," Brianna informed them quietly. "She's cried, she's remembered the good times and shared them with us. While she was nursing the baby a short while ago, she was talking about the future. It won't be easy for her—" Brianna's eyes sought out her husband's "—but she has the advantage of belonging to a terrific family."

"Amen to that," Jess proclaimed.

Luke watched the wordless exchange between his brother and his wife. Their silent communication was touching, the love between them shown for all to see.

He'd wanted that kind of relationship. It was exactly what Maggie had rejected . . . and what Sara had lost to a sniper's bullet.

"Are you going to join us downstairs or continue to mourn in private?" Jess inquired, his arm hooked possessively over his wife's small shoulders.

"Guess I should join the rest, huh?"

"Unless you'd do better discussing your feelings with the friend you mentioned," Jess suggested.

"What friend?" Brianna asked.

"Luke has a friend who lost a family member. Brother, was it?"

"Yeah. Brother."

"Do we know him?" Brianna questioned.

Luke stared past her to Jess.

"Or is it a woman?" his brother guessed.

Luke nodded.

"I have the distinct feeling I'm missing something important," Brianna said. "Do you guys know what it's like to come in in the middle of the movie? Uh-oh. I've seen that look before. You want me to leave. Okay, I'm gone. Join me downstairs after," she offered, looking meaningfully from one to the other. Without another word, she left the room.

Luke walked back to the window and leaned his head against the pane. Outside, the breeze whipped through the trees. He heard the clatter of branches knocking together. He watched the towering pines sway under the strength of the wind.

He didn't have to wait long for Jess to continue his interrogation.

"Tell me about your friend," Jess instructed. "I'll make myself comfortable on your bed. We aren't going anywhere, you know. You may as well tell me. Is she brunette?"

"Blond," Luke muttered.

"Blond. That's a switch." There was a curious but amused note in Jess MacLaren's deep voice. "Is she attractive?"

"Beautiful."

"Beautiful and blond. All right. That's a start," Jess acknowledged. "A beautiful, blond friend. Is this a serious relationship?"

Luke shook his head and concentrated on the world outside his window.

"So it's casual," Jess continued. "See very much of her?"

"Yeah," he answered curtly.

"What does she do?" Jess asked.

Luke glanced over his shoulder. Jess was stretched out on the bed with his hands linked behind his head and his legs crossed at his ankles. He appeared relaxed—and amused. "Third degree, counselor?"

"Yes, sir! Pretend I'm your big brother and I'm trying to be helpful. That way this line of questioning won't seem quite so personal," he joked.

"Sure, counselor. Whatever you say."

"Do you sleep with her, Luke?"

"Yeah," he confessed somewhat reluctantly. "I sleep with her."

"Aha!"

"Aha, yourself."

"We have a beautiful, blond, *casual* friend we sleep with. Interesting."

"Where are you going with this?"

"Just considering the facts, little brother," he said. "You haven't been involved with anyone, to my knowledge, since Maggie left. You seemed to handle her presence at the services this morning quite well."

Now Luke spun to face his brother. "I'm not *involved* with anyone!" he bit out.

"You sleep with her. That's not involved?"

"It's just sex," Luke mumbled.

"I see." Jess didn't look as if he believed him. "Is this, by any chance, the same woman who delayed our fishing trip?"

"Yeah. What's your point, counselor?

"How do you feel about Maggie?"

"This morning I was more concerned with Sara's loss than Maggie's presence."

"But," Jess reminded him, "you stayed with her."

"Ted was *our* friend. She was feeling the loss as much as I was."

"Did you feel protective?"

"Yeah, of course I did," he replied. "Old habits die hard. But Maggie doesn't want my protection. I'm not even sure she wants my friendship," he admitted. "Ex-lovers, in this case, don't make good friends. What she needed today was someone to lean on or someone to hold her up. Whichever."

"And you gallantly offered the needed service."

"What would you have done?"

"Probably the very same thing."

"Great! I made the right move."

Jess gestured expressively, as if to say, *Maybe, maybe not.* "What next?" he inquired. "Is Maggie off again?"

"What Maggie does, big brother, is *not* my concern. No mention was made of what used to be Maggie and Luke. We talked about Ted and Sara."

"I see."

"Do you?" he challenged. "Do you know how I felt? The woman I wanted to marry stood by my side for hours today, leaned on me, cried on me, and not once, *not once* did she allude to the fact that we'd ever shared anything special. She used me today. She assumed I'd be there for her. I always have." He shook his head, feeling something closer to disgust than hurt.

"You know, big brother, she didn't bother to inquire as to how I was doing. She asked nothing personal. She treated me like . . . Sara's brother. Nothing more. And yet she touched me, held my arm, put her head on my shoulder and sobbed . . . as if it were as natural as breathing. Do you know how awkward that was for me?"

"You do realize she's probably been using you like that for a long time?"

Luke sighed quietly. "Yeah. I'd already guessed as much."

"You referred to her as the woman you *wanted* to marry," Jess pointed out.

"Yeah? Maybe that's exactly what I meant. Wanted, as in the past."

"Perhaps your beautiful friend has something to do with that?"

"Yeah," Luke conceded. "We talk sometimes . . . and she meets my physical needs, as well as supplying a . . . closeness. I'm not ready for any emotional involvement."

"Playing around is not going to satisfy you, Luke. You've always planned on marriage and family."

"Maggie's departure destroyed my plans and expectations."

"Give yourself time, Luke. Don't lock yourself away from feeling. That's no way to accomplish healing."

"Maybe not. But it prevents the hurt. . . ."

As the day wore on, Luke sank deeper into depression. Early in the evening he sat in the den talking with his brother Drew and their friend Rand. But they were discussing happier times, and Luke could find no joy in anything. He felt isolated, separate from them, so he retreated to the privacy of his tower room to grieve alone.

He still carried the drink Drew had poured for him. He'd tasted it, felt the smooth fire sliding down his throat, but he hadn't wanted more.

He didn't know what he wanted. A return to normal, whatever it was, would be a start. But that was impossible. Ted wasn't coming back. Luke knew he had to accept that, hard though it may be.

The tower room echoed with emptiness. Luke had thought he wanted to be alone, but he couldn't bear that, either. The silence in the room seemed to smother him.

He felt numb inside—almost like being chilled from the cold.

He took another sip of scotch, but it did not satisfy his need. Glaring at the half-full glass, he put it on the dresser and snatched up his keys.

He needed Mandy—needed her understanding and her warmth. He wanted to hold on to her, lose himself in her until his desperate hunger for warmth abated. Until the anguish and despair were driven from his mind and he could forget the days behind him.

Mandy woke alone the next morning, instantly aware of Luke's absence. It wasn't like him to leave without saying good-bye. But then, last night had been different than most.

For a while she lay still, staring at the ceiling, thinking back over the previous evening, wondering what she would say to him when they came face-to-face.

When he'd pulled her into his arms, she had smelled alcohol on his breath. And even though she'd cringed inwardly at the memories the odor provoked, she hadn't been able to deny Luke. He'd made his desire known, much as he always did. Yet he had displayed none of his customary caring. He'd taken from her and, still holding her close, fallen asleep.

When she sat up she spied Luke's scruffy Reeboks on the floor next to the closet. She closed her eyes and sighed deeply, accepting the tug she felt and the relief that swept through her at the sight of those old shoes.

He hadn't left. And that meant she'd have the chance to talk with him, console him, and try to understand what he was feeling.

She found him sitting in the living room. As she fastened the belt of her robe, she stared at him. "I'm glad you're still here."

"I'm hard to lose," he muttered. He raised his head slowly, impaling her with saddened, murky green eyes. "I'm sorry about last night, Mandy. That's no way to treat a friend."

"I . . ." she began. "I've put it behind me."

"Great," was his sullen response.

Mandy studied his brooding expression, trying to determine the best way to approach him this morning. "Are you hungry?"

"I made coffee," he returned.

"If you're hungry, I'll fix—"

"Don't bother."

"It's no bother, really."

"I can't eat, Mandy. No appetite. I'm . . . numb."

She seated herself on the edge of the sofa facing him. "I remember the feeling. When Ben died I lost days, weeks, living a zombie-like existence."

"How did you—" He stopped, and then shook his head, rubbing his hand over the back of his neck. "I feel like I've been . . . mutilated. Like part of me is gone . . . or lost." He glanced at her as if to say, *Do you understand*? "How did you go on with your life?"

"It took time. We all grieve in our own way . . . and mend in our own way."

"Mend," he spat out angrily. "Yeah, sure. I'm gonna need one hell of a bandage."

"We can talk to each other, Luke. I've been where you are. I know how you're feeling," she sympathized.

Luke exhaled loudly. "Do you?" he challenged. "My sister has two children. Megan is not quite two and Molly is only six months. Those sweet, innocent little girls will never know their daddy. . . ." He swallowed hard, trying to hold the desolate feeling at bay.

Mandy watched, aware of the tension building as he spoke. She'd never seen this side of Luke. His posture was rigid—so unnatural for him. She sensed strong emotions hovering close to the surface, without the benefit of his customary casual veneer to cover them.

"All because the courts let this criminally insane person loose on our streets. He took the lives of seven nameless, faceless people. Called them sitting ducks!" Luke paused to suck in a long breath of air, then let it go slowly. "But they weren't nameless or faceless to anyone, only in his sick mind. They were living, breathing, loving, productive members of society. Each of them had families. . . . Did you hear how many kids that killer orphaned? Five children lost both parents. Three others witnessed the slaughter. Imagine watching your mom or dad murdered. . . . Imagine witnessing that violence through a child's eyes."

"It's not something I'd want to see firsthand as an adult," she said solemnly.

"Yeah, right. But the people in that restaurant weren't given a choice. God!" He rubbed his hand across his neck again.

"Luke, I understand your need to talk about this. I know you're hurting and upset with the injustice of an irrational act, but perhaps you shouldn't dwell on the . . . horror."

He raised his eyes to meet hers. "What do you mean?" His voice held an odd sort of challenge. It put

Mandy on the defensive. This type of conversation simply was not the norm for the two of them.

"Don't try to reconstruct the scene and imagine thoughts and feelings—"

"I can't help what I'm thinking and feeling!"

"I understand the agony—"

"Sure you do," he interrupted sarcastically.

Mandy held her tongue. Sometimes words weren't appropriate. If she could find the patience to withhold her own thoughts and simply listen without interjecting comments, perhaps he'd be better off. What he needed was someone to listen.

"Tell me what you're thinking," she coaxed.

"What I'm thinking," he bit out, "is that sharing my thoughts with anyone is futile. It won't bring Ted back. It won't bring back the other victims, either. Thinking, talking, none of it will alter what has happened this week. No matter what Luke MacLaren thinks or feels or says . . . it doesn't make any difference. Nothing makes any difference in the end. Nothing!" he emphasized angrily. "I could use a drink!"

"How about breakfast," she countered. "You need to eat."

"You don't know what I need, lady," he returned sharply. "I need to forget and I need a drink!"

"You know very well there's nothing here to drink."

Glaring at her, he rose abruptly from the large, overstuffed chair. "Yeah. Guess there's no reason for me to hang around." He disappeared into the bedroom for only a minute, then stalked toward the door, wrenching it open in one swift angry movement.

Mandy managed to blurt out a feeble "Luke" before the door slammed behind him.

She was stunned. Grief and anger had transformed her carefree, likable lover into—what was that phrase he had used?—an inconsiderate bastard. Uncaring. Unfeeling.

No, she realized, the problem was that he felt deeply, too deeply. Pain had created an angry monster she didn't recognize.

Mandy was heartsick. It had taken days for him to return, and when he did, she hadn't given him the comfort he needed. She had failed him, and now she feared she had run out of chances.

SIX

While she worked, Mandy couldn't help remembering snatches of the past twenty-four hours. Initially she blamed herself for making a mess of the situation, for not being sensitive enough, or caring enough, or whatever it was she had done to drive him away. And then she came to her senses. It had not been her fault. Luke was grieving. He was angry, hurting, and irrational. He came to her wanting physical satisfaction. He hadn't awakened her with warm, tender kisses as was his habit, hadn't even spoken to her. He'd used her, satisfied himself, and fallen asleep.

She'd realized at the time something was very wrong. The gentle, caring lover she knew seemed like a stranger. He had not soared into ecstasy with her or showered her with soft kisses afterward, although he had clutched her to his side as he'd drifted off to sleep. She had given. Luke had taken. They hadn't shared. That was wrong—and incredibly sad. Luke needed someone, especially now, to share with him. She wanted to be that someone.

She knew he was wrapped too deeply in his own

feelings, his own despair, to reach out to her. She would have to find a way to reach out to him. The question was how?

As the day progressed, her mind frequently returned to the problem of how to touch Luke. She was certain he wouldn't stop by that evening. Anger between them was new, untried, and somehow, she realized, would only bring forth his armor, not his customary good sense.

She sat alone in her kitchen that evening, eating a pizza and pondering the problem. She thought she knew Luke MacLaren well. He had kept to himself or walled up with his family for days. When he had sought her out, the outcome had been disastrous.

Once again she reflected on their final words that morning. Luke wanted a drink. And his kisses had carried a hint of alcohol the night before. . . .

Memories of her father loomed before her. She knew Luke wasn't like him, and yet the way he'd looked when he insisted he *needed* to forget . . .

No, Luke, she cried silently. *Please no*.

Hoping she was wrong, but on the chance she wasn't, Mandy marched into the bathroom to freshen up before going to search for him.

An hour later Mandy walked into the crowded barroom. It was smoky, smelly, and loud. She'd never liked coming here with Amy, and she didn't like it now. She felt decidedly out of place as she stood in the doorway studying the patrons, searching for one familiar face. Several moments passed before she spotted him. He was sitting at the bar. She was thankful he was alone.

That had been a major concern. She feared he might look elsewhere—to another's arms—for solace. She edged her way around the tables, past the small groups of people, feeling self-conscious and out of place, but determinedly keeping her goal in sight. She had to reach Luke somehow. Had to show him that alcohol was not the anesthetic he wanted it to be.

Mandy eased herself onto the bar stool next to him, clutching her small handbag in her lap. He sat with his forearms on the bar, supporting the weight of his upper body.

She gave his relaxed form a quick once-over, then touched his arm lightly with her fingertips.

Before she even spoke, he muttered, "What's a nice girl like you doing in a place like this?"

"Looking for a friend," she replied. "Is that your line or did you realize it was me?"

"I recognize the perfume," he told her, still not looking up. "I sleep with it. I mean . . . the lady I sleep with wears it to bed."

"I'm flattered you noticed," she remarked quietly.

"Yeah . . ." He turned to her, deep lines of despair etching his handsome face.

"Need a friend?"

"Why'd you come here, lady?"

"I was looking for a friend," she repeated.

"For sex?' he asked, hanging his head. "Your lover let you down last night. Ought to be plenty of guys willing to—"

"Stop it. Friends don't destroy each other with accusations. Friends don't impose their judgmental attitudes on each other. We aren't merely lovers, Luke. We *are* friends. . . . Aren't we?"

He nodded. "Yeah, friends."

"I'm sorry, Luke," she began. "I'm afraid I—"

"Wait. Wait," he rasped, holding up a hand to silence her. "What the hell are you sorry for? You don't have any reason to apologize."

"I allowed memories of my father to color my attitude—"

"Oh, Mandy." He reached to pull her against him. For long moments he simply held her close. "Sweet angel," he murmured, smothering her mouth with his hungry kiss.

"I thought—" she started to say. But Luke prevented any words from escaping as he captured her lips with his again.

"Yeah," he muttered against her mouth. "What'd you think?"

"That you might need a friend to listen to you, to be with you," she finished.

"Just to be with me?"

"Yeah," was her soft reply.

"Yeah," he acknowledged. "I do. And I'd kind of like to be with you right now, but," he took a deep breath, then released it slowly, "I can't."

Mandy swallowed hard. Her stomach knotted with tension. "You've made other plans?" She forced out the words, trying her utmost to sound casual.

"Yeah . . ." He chuckled.

She tensed even more, finding no humor in his reply.

"You see, sweet lady," he said. "Mom declared the house off limits for the evening. Said her home was not a mausoleum and everyone should get out for a while. My brothers wouldn't allow me to be alone. They *encouraged* me to join them here."

"They're here?" Relief washed through Mandy in great sweeping waves.

"Yeah," he grinned. "In the other room playing pool. I play the winner."

"Lucky you." She smiled to herself.

He touched a finger to her lips. "I'm sorry, Mandy. I let you down last night."

Raising her eyes, Mandy studied him carefully. His

face was drawn and tired-looking. His hair was as tousled as if he just gotten out of bed. His eyelids were drooping.

"You're a sight," she whispered, reaching a hand to nudge a lock of hair from his forehead. "You should go home and get some sleep."

"Mandy." He drew her into his arms again. When his hold loosened, she sat back on her chair. Spying his drink she reached over, moving the glass out of his way.

He raised his eyebrows in mock surprise, then shrugged his shoulders and grinned broadly. "It's just ginger ale."

She picked it up and took a sip. "It's flat."

"Yeah, well, I guess I stirred it until the fizz was gone. I was thinking about you."

"Nice thoughts, I hope."

"I want to apologize for walking out on you this morning. I wasn't angry with you. I just haven't figured out how to handle my grief."

"Did you . . . find that drink you wanted so desperately?"

"Yeah. Black coffee. I made it a double. I was going to come back with breakfast, but I decided I wouldn't be good company. You deserve better."

"I'll be the judge of that, MacLaren."

"Thanks, friend," he said. "Would you like a Perrier?"

Mandy shook her head. "I'll let you get back to your brothers." Something made her glance over her shoulder. Not one, but two MacLarens stood a short distance from them, watching.

"Their game must have ended. They've come looking for you." As she slipped off the bar stool, Luke caught her by the shoulder and pulled her close again. His kiss was a tender apology, yet it fueled her desire.

Reluctantly, she eased away, running her tongue over her lips to savor the taste of him. Filled with suppressed longing, she caressed his jaw lovingly, then turned and walked away.

The next day, Mandy's thoughts wandered repeatedly to Luke. She realized that happened more and more as time passed. She still hadn't come up with a way to break through his self-pity and help him see beyond this crisis. She believed she'd have a better chance if he'd return to his previous routine and spend time with her. But if he didn't, her chances were slim. To take her mind off Luke, she grabbed a book and stretched out on the couch to read.

It proved to be an exercise in futility. She couldn't concentrate, as thoughts of Luke superimposed themselves on the story. And, too, she was exhausted—mentally and emotionally. Several times she dozed off, only to wake herself when her head nodded onto her chest.

Something else awakened her now. Something that sounded like the key. But when she glanced at the door, it had not opened. She rubbed her eyes, then pulled herself into a sitting position, staring blurry-eyed at the closed door. She blinked, then realizing the lock had turned, let go of the breath she'd been holding.

Someone was fumbling with the knob. It had to be Luke. He was the only person who had a key for the deadbolt.

At long last the door swung open and he came into view.

"Hi." He grinned, spying her on the couch. "Wake you?"

"I guess I fell asleep reading," she explained while he closed the door and locked it again.

"I haven't been able to sleep," he announced. "Every time I close my eyes, I see the headlines . . ."

Mandy rose and walked slowly toward him, assessing his appearance. He seemed so tired. Was the lover she knew hidden somewhere beneath that mantle of weariness? "You look like hell."

"Worse, probably."

As she wrapped her arm around his waist, she felt his weight shift onto her. "I don't think you ought to drive—"

"I called a cab."

"Why didn't you call me?"

"I . . . wasn't sure . . ." he began. "I didn't know if you'd really forgiven me for acting like a jerk the other night." He reached out to caress her short hair with his strong hand. "I thought if I just showed up, you wouldn't throw me out."

"Yeah," she teased. "I'm a real sucker—"

"Damn, Mandy," he groaned. "I'm sorry."

"Come on over to the couch," she ordered. "I'm not going to stand here all night holding you up."

"Is the bedroom off limits?"

"No. Of course not."

"I need to lie down, Mandy."

"Okay, we'll head for the bed. Just put one foot in front of the other and we'll get there . . . eventually," she added as an afterthought.

"I'm so tired," he confessed. "Drained . . ."

"So we'll tuck you in bed and let you sleep off the tired. Your body's probably protesting the abuse it's taken recently."

Mandy guided him carefully into the bedroom. Once there, she administered a playful, but well-placed nudge and he landed, none too gently, sprawled over the mattress.

He looked so surprised, she laughed. "Sorry. I couldn't resist the urge."

"Funny lady," he growled. "Help me undress? I don't think I have the strength to loosen one damn button."

"Poor baby." She sat next to him and reached to unbutton his green plaid shirt.

"Sympathetic by nature?"

"I never learned to enjoy undressing—" Mandy caught herself just in time. She had almost equated him with her father. And Luke wasn't at all like her dad. She'd apologized for that mistake last night and here she was lumping Luke into that category again.

One hand encircled her waist, pulling her against him. His other hand reached out to her soft hair, tenderly stroking.

"Make me some coffee?" he asked quietly.

"And who'll undress you?"

"Details . . . details . . ."

"First I'll undress you, then if you still want coffee, I'll make some decaf, so you can sleep."

"Thanks," he murmured. He lay still as she finished unbuttoning his shirt, unbuckled his belt, unzipped his pants, and removed his socks and shoes.

"Are you still conscious?" she whispered.

"Barely."

"I'll need your cooperation if you want to get out of these clothes." She leaned across his wide frame and placed one hand on each side of his waist. "Lift those cute buns, MacLaren," she ordered, winking as he raised languid but astonished eyes to meet hers. She tugged at the denim of his jeans until they were around his knees. "Okay, now do you think you can raise your big feet off the bed?"

"Piece of cake," he mumbled, obeying her command.

"No cake until you're one hundred percent conscious,'' she returned. She felt a light chuckle ripple through his body. ''Hey, MacLaren, you're going to have to sit for a minute while I relieve you of your shirt.''

Luke sighed long and loud. ''Sit? As in up? You've got to be kidding. This body—''

''Had better cooperate,'' she finished for him. ''Up!''

He groaned, then braced himself with one hand and slowly, awkwardly, levered himself to a sitting position.

Mandy slipped her hands under the fabric of his shirt and pushed it off his broad shoulders, her hands lingering longer than necessary on his bare skin.

The caressing gesture did not go unnoticed. ''Later,'' he promised, placing a gentle kiss on her forehead. ''After the coffee.''

''Didn't I say decaf?'' she reminded him. ''You need sleep.''

''I didn't say how much later,'' he murmured, lowering himself against the pillow.

''No, you didn't.'' Mandy grinned as she watched him relax on the bed. ''I'll make the coffee.''

Mandy was wide awake, refreshed after her short nap. As she prepared the coffee maker, she hummed to herself. Luke had come back to her of his own accord. She smiled contentedly. She was concerned by his appearance, concerned for his physical well-being. But she had told herself she wouldn't judge him. The phrase ''until you've walked in someone else's shoes'' ran through her mind. He had to deal with his grief, face reality in his own way. All she could do was offer her friendship and be there for him when he needed her.

Mandy sliced some ham and cheese, rinsed some lettuce, and made two sandwiches. Chances were he wasn't hungry, but she'd offer, just in case. She fixed the tray they always used for their intimate breakfasts or midnight snacks. Plates, napkins, mugs, coffee carafe. She was ready.

She giggled as she walked toward the bedroom. Carrying coffee to a man who had more than likely fallen asleep—and here she was dressed like a hooker. She had forgotten how little she wore. He was probably too fatigued to notice, though he had commented "later" when she hadn't been able to refrain from touching his warm flesh. Well, coffee, sandwiches, and his favorite dessert, she mused, ought to distract him for a while.

"Coffee," she whispered in his ear.

Luke raised his drowsy eyelids and gazed deep into Mandy's aquamarine eyes. "Smells good. Thanks."

When he levered himself up onto the pillows and reached out his hand, she placed the hot mug within his grasp.

"You're not going to spill that, are you?"

A crooked smile spread slowly across his face. "You won't let me, will you?"

"Want me to hold it steady while you sip?"

"Yeah." Luke folded his large hand over Mandy's smaller one, possessively, then took a few sips of the steaming liquid. "Delicious," he pronounced.

She watched as he leaned toward the mug again.

"Thanks, friend," he told her.

Nodding an acknowledgment, she reached up, lovingly brushing back a stray lock of hair from his forehead.

He smiled and sucked in a deep breath. "I tried to forget . . . Ted," he began, his voice hushed. "I can't. Nothing dulls the memories. They linger on and on. When I close my eyes, his death haunts me. It keeps me awake. And when I do sleep, each time I wake, the sadness, the memories return." He took another sip of coffee. "So I start all over, trying to forget. Nothing works, Mandy. I can't seem to forget."

"You don't have to forget your feelings or your friendship with Ted," she explained in a soft voice. "You don't have to forget Ted or how he died. You merely have to accept that he's gone and go on with your own life. Keep the good memories. Hold them in your heart and nurture them. You can still love Ted, still treasure his friendship. The part of your life he shared is part of you." She ran her fingertips lightly along Luke's wrist.

"Perhaps you should find a way to channel your feelings. Find some direction, some new purpose. Something different to hold your interest until the hurt is not so new."

"Like what?" His eyes pleaded with her.

"I don't know. I don't have all the answers. I'm merely making suggestions. There must be something you've wanted to do, but never found time for."

"Is that what you did when Ben died?"

"In a manner of speaking."

"What was it that you tried?"

Mandy hesitated. "After weeks and weeks of despondency, I was forced to re-evaluate my negative outlook on life." She paused thoughtfully, taking a sip of coffee from her mug, then turning to place it on the nightstand. She glanced at Luke to find him studying her.

"And?" he prompted. "What was it that goaded you out of despondency?"

"David. He was not happy with my outlook on life. He reminded me that all the crying in the world wasn't going to bring Ben back. He told me I was absolutely no good to anyone locked away in my room. I was wasting my life—and making a hell of his. He informed me that *he* was alive and well, and I had better open my eyes and start treating him like a husband, or else.''

''Or else?'' Luke echoed curiously.

''He'd leave. Find someone who was capable of functioning as a wife.''

''God, Mandy.''

''He was right.'' She continued in spite of the look on Luke's face. ''I hadn't considered his feelings of neglect. I'd only looked inward. I was so devastated by Ben's illness and his death, that I . . . didn't make any time for my husband.'' She paused, unconsciously chewing on her bottom lip. ''The argument forced me to look at our relationship. I knew I wanted more from marriage than I had at that time, and I believed a great deal of fault lay on my part. Oh, David was a taker, true enough, but I'd given him very little as Ben's condition deteriorated. I wasn't involved with my marriage enough to care that we'd become nothing more than roommates. Two people living in the same dwelling. Our lives didn't even parallel.'' She stopped, staring blankly at the wall, remembering.

Running one long finger along her spine, Luke commented, ''That doesn't sound like the Mandy I know.''

She shivered, glanced over her shoulder, and smiled at him. ''No, I don't suppose it does. But my brother was very special.'' Tears welled up in her eyes. She swallowed hard to hold back her emotions. ''Anyway, I got my act together. I decided to be the best wife ever. David would never have any cause to leave me because I was determined to be every bit as perfect as he wanted. Our home was a showplace—attractive, inviting, and immaculate. I prepared elegant, candle-light dinners for him—always gourmet, of course—and made sure I was available to him whenever he wanted. I tried to return to my job for a few hours a week, in spite of the fact David didn't approve. Scheduling that was the one source of conflict between us.''

"But in spite of your efforts, the marriage failed," Luke said.

"Well, yes, it did," she acknowledged. "Many months later. The point is, having some direction brought me out of my despair."

"And if you can do it, so can I? Is that the logic involved here?"

She nodded. "Exactly what I was thinking."

"Plausible theory . . ."

"Do I detect a 'but it'll never work' attitude, MacLaren?"

"Yeah," he admitted. "I didn't say I wouldn't give the idea some thought. It's only that I'm having some difficulty with my rational thinking process tonight."

"You ought to try to sleep."

Luke positioned his muscular frame beside hers, folding his arms beneath his head and staring off at the ceiling. "Yeah. I'm not doing myself any good. I can't bring Ted back. And I'm not doing my sister any good. I ought to be around for her to lean on. I ought to help her with the girls," he said thoughtfully. "You like kids?"

"Sure, I like kids."

"Why didn't you and your husband—" he began. "Never mind. None of my business."

"We tried. We weren't successful," she revealed, purposely not elaborating.

"Oh," he muttered lamely. "Sara and Ted were married three years before they tried, and they were quite successful." Luke chuckled. "Matter of fact, if you think about it, my family's got a fantastic success rate. Mom and Dad have the six of us, Jess and Brianna have been blessed twice. And there are a bunch of MacLaren cousins."

"Family," she said in reverent tones. "It's everything to you."

Luke drew in a long, weary breath. "It's a very large part of my life, Mandy. We've always been involved with one another, and not to the exclusion of friends. We got involved in school, in sports, in community activities, in church—always with the love, approval, and support of our family. Jess shocked us all when he chose to study law away from home. We questioned his wisdom but stood by his decision. Everyone of us worries about Drew each time he flies off on one of his crusades to save the world. But we love him, respect his beliefs and his decision to make a difference somehow. Our family unit is strong, secure, an integral part of each of us. Brianna was saying after the services that one of the best things about being a MacLaren is that we have each other, we're never alone."

"I envy you, you know. I don't have that sense of family . . . never had it. It seems beautiful . . . warm."

Silent green eyes studied her. "It is," he said. "It's all that and more." He smiled, one corner of his mouth turned up slightly higher than the other. "*You* are beautiful, Amanda Burke," he whispered. His gaze roamed freely over her scantily clad body. "And if you wiggle over here close to me, lady, I'll make you warm."

"That's a hard invitation to refuse," she murmured, inching closer.

"Let me hold you. Let me wrap my arms around you and keep you safe and warm while we sleep."

"Sounds like heaven."

"Yeah, heaven." He drew her into his arms, enfolded her securely alongside him, and closed his eyes.

In a matter of minutes, Mandy realized he was asleep, relaxed, breathing deeply, but still holding her. She was contented. They often slept entwined. Tonight was different because there had been no passionate physical union, yet she felt as satisfied lying with him now as if there had been.

They had shared their feelings instead of their bodies. She'd shown him she cared about him and about what he did with his life. And he had exposed another layer of himself, telling her how useless he felt in the face of despair. He had emphasized again how thankful he was to belong to his family. In the wake of that revelation, he had brought her closer, warmed her with his smile and his caring actions. There had been a union between them, she realized. That was the source of the satisfaction running through her. Emotional union with the man whose heart beat next to hers. It was beautiful, so beautiful.

Mandy slept.

Something tickled. She moaned softly in her sleep, trying to identify the problem. Something warm was making patterns on her stomach. She took a sleepy swipe at it with her hand, only to have her hand captured and held.

Mandy fought her way from the depths of slumber. A finger, a very warm finger, was tracing delicate paths across her body. Her captive hand was being kissed, licked, and sucked upon.

Luke.

She dared to open one drowsy lid.

"This provocative little red number is new, isn't it?" he asked, grinning suggestively.

She groaned.

"I can't sleep, Mandy," he whispered. "Please wake up. I need you."

She responded instinctively to the obvious need in his voice. She wiggled and turned until her body was lying flush with his and she could feel his arousal against her abdomen.

"You're . . . naked," she murmured.

"I am," he chuckled. "I'm naked, awake . . . and much, much more than willing." The words hung suspended in the air.

"Mmm," she practically purred, pressing against him. "What are you waiting for, MacLaren," she whispered. "Take me."

His agile fingers trailed down her back with tantalizing sureness. "Help me remove this enticing bit of lingerie, you wanton woman," he instructed as he cupped her firm derriere.

"Why don't you try to remove it all by yourself," she challenged.

"Oh, so it's that way, is it? Going to be difficult and uncooperative?"

"Nooo," she drawled. "Merely heightening the anticipation.

"Ah! You want me to explore every inch of you? Withhold satisfaction?"

"I'd never encourage teasing," she informed him. "Nor would I want you to become so accustomed to my charms as to demand and expect immediate gratification."

Luke stared down at her, a knowing gleam in his eyes. With amazing slowness he brought his hand to rest on her breast. He traced circles around her taut nipple, once, twice, three times. Tantalizing. Finally, he grasped it firmly between his thumb and forefinger and tugged gently. He watched her eyes darken with pleasure, then close. He trailed his fingers to the other breast, repeating the action.

Once again Mandy moaned with pleasure. He increased his assault to her senses, first exploring her sensitive skin with his hands, and then with his lips and mouth. She was pliant beneath him, aching for his masterful touch, desiring his possession of her, unable to focus on anything more than the delightful sensations that were flowing through every thoroughly aroused inch of her body.

And still he continued, prolonging his intimate ministrations—touching her, tasting her, at last discovering how to remove the frivolous apparel that had tantalized him upon waking. Deftly he removed the fabric from her heated flesh, then proceeded with his sensual foreplay.

He discovered she was not only willing, but hot, moist, and ready. He ravished her with impassioned kisses, still refraining from the movement that would bring them both satisfaction. His broad body pinned her to the bed, her silken skin so close to his it felt like a glove. He kissed her again and again, savoring each kiss, making each touch of their lips memorable, separate from the next.

She writhed beneath him, wrapping her legs around his waist, silently begging him to hasten their joining. He groaned against her pliant lips as her legs tightened around him.

"Now," he rasped, finally giving in to the pleasure.

It was all she had expected and more. Everything his silent ministrations had promised. They became one—mind, body, and soul united in ecstasy.

"Good morning," he whispered in her ear.

She touched his face, caressing his cheek with her dainty fingers. "Good morning, Luke," she murmured.

"You're some kind of friend," he commented, his tone casual.

But she knew he meant what he had said. She knew, too, that what was unspoken was implied. She assumed he meant to keep it light.

"Thank you," she remarked, playfully adding, "I found the experience pleasurable also."

"Yeah?" he countered soberly. "I'm willing to admit that was a bit more than great sex, Mandy. How about it?"

She was instantly aware of the hint of sobriety in his tone. When she peered up at him, his eyes were stormy. Mandy bit her lip, then weighed her words before she spoke.

"I'm sorry. I thought you wanted to keep it light. You aren't normally inclined to . . . analyze the level of . . . pleasure we give each other." She paused, bringing one slender finger to his lips. "I feel complete with you," she confessed softly, "and beautiful and warm and secure. You give so much of yourself. I feel as if I'm wrapped so tightly to you that I'm an inseparable part of you."

"Yeah," he whispered. "You're part of me. You give me just as much, lady. Each time you take me inside, you give me a piece of yourself that's only mine."

"Perceptive," she commented.

"Maybe . . ." He hesitated. "I think what we share heightens that perception or sensitivity, whatever it is that adds dimension to our union."

They stared deep into each other's eyes as if they were trying to read the other's mind, as if they could find explanations for why their relationship had reached this point and brought them both a strange knowledge of the other.

Then Luke smiled. And Mandy silently acknowledged that smile. It was more than devastating. It lit his entire face, made his eyes sparkle, brilliant green orbs dancing with happiness and a peace she'd never read in their depths before.

"You're okay, MacLaren."

"I'm okay, Amanda Burke," he returned.

"Time to get back to the routine?" she questioned tentatively.

"Need to spend some time with my sister and her kids," he decided. "But then I believe I'll fall right back into the same routine, with a few important alterations."

"Such as?"

"Spending more time with Sara, and—" he cleared his throat "—more time with you."

She smiled. "I'd like that."

"Yeah . . . me, too," he agreed, still bestowing that smile on her. "Have time for a quick, stimulating shower?"

"Who could refuse that invitation?" she tossed back at him as she scampered off the bed and dashed toward the bathroom.

SEVEN

As Luke sauntered into the den of his parents' home he watched his older brother fill a glass with a generous amount of ice and carefully pour a small quantity of scotch over the cubes.

"Hello, stranger," Jess greeted him. He capped the bottle of scotch and replaced it in the well-stocked liquor cabinet. "Mom said you seem to be getting back to normal again. Where have you been hiding?"

"I've been holed up with Sara, playing with Megan and helping with Molly. Sara and I were talking. We decided to make new memories together." Luke sprawled casually in an overstuffed rocker, swinging one leg over the arm of the chair.

"Sounds like a good start." Jess nodded in agreement. "She's doing well, isn't she?"

"Yeah," Luke admitted. "A lot better than I am."

"Where have you been?" Jess asked again.

"Out."

"Obviously. You missed dinner the past two nights. It hasn't escaped my notice. Neither has the fact that your bed hasn't been slept in."

"Checking up on me, big brother?" Luke's eyebrows knit together as he glanced toward his sibling. He stroked his mustache with his thumb and forefinger.

"Keeping tabs on you. I believe that's what big brothers are supposed to do."

"Yeah, right."

"It seems to me if you haven't been home and you haven't been with us, then you must have been with your beautiful friend," Jess guessed.

"Yeah," Luke admitted reluctantly.

"And do you feel better?"

"Yeah. She fought her way up from the bottom when her brother died. She says she knows how I feel. . . . Maybe she does," he allowed, shrugging his shoulders.

"Why don't you bring the lady home to meet the family?" Jess suggested.

"No," Luke emphatically refused.

"Why not?"

"This family is mourning. This is not the time to bring a casual friend home for a visit."

Jess plunked the glass onto the coffee table and turned his full attention to Luke. "The family is not dead. It has not ceased to function as a unit because one member is gone. Our friends have always been welcome here, good times or bad. You seem to rely on this lady's friendship. I'd like to meet her. I'm sure the others would welcome a change."

"No!" Luke repeated, sitting upright in his chair. "I'm not bringing her home. I can have friends without having your approval, can't I?"

"I'm not suggesting anyone pass approval on your friend, Luke. What's wrong with introducing her to the family?"

Luke leaned his head back against the cushion and closed his eyes. "You've misinterpreted the relationship," he declared, wondering how to explain his situation. He had always looked up to his older brother. And while Jess might teasingly suggest that Luke find a woman, he, himself, would never indulge in a casual physical relationship. He would, in fact, experience difficulty understanding such a relationship. Jess was a man of honor and commitment, with a strong sense of self-worth and direction.

Luke decided the best approach was to be frank. He wasn't accustomed to keeping secrets from his brother anyway. Maybe Jess wouldn't understand, but he'd lay it on the line. Big brother could deal with cold, hard facts.

"I . . . sleep with her," Luke revealed, watching the expression on the other man's face darken.

"You admitted that the other day," Jess reminded him. "What you mean is you use her to satisfy your baser desires?"

"Yeah," Luke admitted.

"And don't you consider her a friend?"

"Yeah, she's a friend." Luke's attention was drawn from his brother's challenging stance to the petite figure standing in the doorway.

"You two look awfully somber," Brianna said. "Am I interrupting a deep man-to-man, brother-to-brother conversation?"

"Come in, honey." Jess's voice softened as he urged his wife to join them. "I've been trying to encourage Luke to bring his lady home to meet us."

"That would be nice." Brianna reached to ruffle Luke's thick hair. "We'd like to meet her."

Luke gave her an acknowledging nod, then scowled at his older brother. "I'm not planning to introduce her to the clan."

Brianna glanced back and forth from the brother standing rigidly with his hands on his hips to the one seated in the rocking chair. Silently she observed the intensity and anger she sensed in both.

"Are you ashamed of her?" Jess suggested.

"No," Luke stated honestly.

"Why are you so reluctant to introduce us?"

"Timing's wrong," he grumbled.

"That's an excuse. When did any of us hesitate to welcome a friend into our home?"

"I said no," Luke snapped.

"I heard what you said," Jess ground out, his ire provoked.

"Jess . . ." Brianna ventured softly.

He raised a hand to silence her. "And I heard what you implied, Luke. She's good enough to sleep with, she's good enough for you to use, but she's not good enough to bring home. She's nothing more to you than your whore, Luke!" he declared in angry tones. "That's why—"

Luke flew out of the chair, fist raised, ready to slug him. As swift as his movements were, Brianna's were even faster. She'd seen Luke's jaw tense as Jess spoke, she'd witnessed his body grow rigid with anger at her husband's words. And in the seconds before Luke unleashed that anger, she had thrown herself in his path.

"No, Luke," she commanded, blocking the thrust of his fist with her words. She turned to her husband as he tried to push her out of the way. "That's enough, Jess. I think you've made your point."

Luke's cold, hard stare was filled with anger. His chest heaved as he fought for control. He didn't speak. It wasn't necessary. The emotions evident in his stormy eyes said it all. Long, wretched moments later, he pivoted and strode quickly from the room.

Brianna let go of the breath she'd been holding. She raised questioning eyes to her husband. "Don't you think you were a bit hard on him?"

Jess, too, released a long sigh. He plowed his fingers through his hair. "Bri," he began, "he speaks of her as his friend in one breath, then in the next tries to tell me it's just sex. Perhaps I was hard on him," he allowed, "but I don't believe Luke's willing to admit how he feels about the lady. Remember, I've seen her. She *is* a lady. Luke knows that. He attempted to defend her honor. Neither of us has taken a shot at the other for years."

"I knew you were baiting him," she stated quietly, "but I think you went too far."

"Fair's fair, blue eyes." He smiled mischievously, then winked at his wife. "After all, he played cupid for us, didn't he?"

Brianna's lips curved upward as she remembered the part Luke had played in their relationship. "In a way, I suppose he did."

"I'm only returning the favor." Jess pulled Brianna into his arms. His head dipped toward hers. "Luke needs that lady. . . ."

Luke stormed out of the house, fury building in his gut. He got into his car, flipped on the tape player, and turned up the volume. Gunning the engine, he backed, recklessly, out the long driveway.

How could his own brother even dare make such an awful accusation about Mandy? Imagine anyone implying—believing—that Amanda Burke was a whore.

He drove without destination or intent, putting miles on his car. When he finally stopped, an hour or so later, he realized he had parked overlooking the family's shipbuilding yard. No surprise. The water beyond, even when peaked with white caps as it was today, was a home place for him. The lapping waves were music to soothe the savage beast.

Although Luke MacLaren was not normally the savage beast he felt like right now. On the surface, he was the jovial family clown, always easygoing, casual, living for today. Jess was always strong, self-assured, and even-tempered. Drew was the intense, opinionated, angry man among the brothers. Drew wouldn't have hesitated to belt Jess as soon as he'd begun his cool analysis of Luke's lady!

And, damn it, Mandy was a lady!

Luke shook his head and lay across the steering wheel. He had reacted more like everyone expected Drew to react. He'd almost struck Jess. Impossible. Jess was not only his much-loved, well-respected older brother, but through their adult years, particularly since Jess's accident, he'd become his best friend. He was the rock he leaned on . . . hell, clung to, when necessary. Today, a few short hours ago, he had raised his fist to slug that same brother.

Why? How could that happen? He loved him. Always would, no matter what. What had gone wrong? He thought back over their conversation. Big brother had pushed—big deal. They had that kind of relationship. There had been times he'd had to give Jess a nudge or two.

Jess had insulted Mandy. True. But *why?* What gave Jess that right? Nothing! Not a damn thing! He didn't even know her.

And that, of course, was the issue. The family wanted to meet her—and he had stubbornly refused.

To Luke, Mandy represented a kind of retreat, his private hideaway. He didn't want to share her. They had created their own special domain, where they were sheltered, protected from the pain of the real world. He didn't want to let intruders in . . . or so he thought.

But what was it Sara had said? "We've got to live in the real world, Luke. We've got Molly and Megan to think of. A child's world may consist largely of make-believe, but an adult has to take control for himself or herself to live in the real world, admit that life isn't always fair or isn't always what we expect it to be. We've got to, Luke, because life is beautiful, but it's short and unpredictable. We ought to make the best of what God has given us."

Maybe Sara was right.

The real world was paved with pain, he thought. And Amanda offered him what? Not merely solace or temporary physical escape. But a way to heal. She made him admit his suffering. She shared hers. She lived in the real world. And, in her own way, she had encouraged him to do the same. He thought he could. Especially after talking with Sara today.

Still, the conversation with Jess hurt more than he cared to admit. Jess had no right to call her names. Maybe that was his own fault, Luke acknowledged. His brother, his best friend, had no way of knowing just how caring a person Mandy was, or what kind of a friend she'd been to him. Perhaps he ought to remedy that. Perhaps, he allowed, Jess was right. He ought to introduce them. He'd have to give the matter serious consideration.

Luke raised his head and studied the shipyards, then leveled his gaze on the water beyond. Once again, Sara's words filled his head. "Life is beautiful, but it's short and unpredictable."

"I need you, Mandy mine," he whispered to the sea. "I need to tell you. . . ."

He started the engine, and this time he backed his car carefully onto the road.

Luke gave a warning rap against the door, then hesitantly pushed it open to let himself into Mandy's apartment. It was early in the day for him to be making an appearance. He didn't want to startle her.

She came from the kitchen to greet him.

"Hi," he said sheepishly. He eyed her mauve-colored business suit. "You were working?"

"I got in a few minutes ago. Thought I'd pop some moussaka in the oven. Are you hungry? You look . . . awful, Luke. Is something wrong?"

"Yeah, something's wrong. I'm not hungry, but I'll force myself to eat your moussaka . . . later." He rubbed his hand across his forehead, then reached out, motioning to Mandy. "Come sit with me," he invited, heavy steps taking him toward the formal sofa.

"Just a second. I'll pop this in the oven."

Less than a minute later, Mandy approached the sofa from the other side, placed her hand in his, then sat, curling herself comfortably next to him.

"I had an argument with my brother," Luke began.

"I assume, as a rule, you don't disagree?"

"Brotherly bantering. Nothing heavy."

"Today was different?" she ventured. "A real argument?"

"Yeah," he admitted in somber tones. Then he fell silent.

"Do you want to tell me about it?" She squeezed his hand gently. Her understanding eyes invited him to share his feelings.

Releasing his breath little by little, he nodded.

"Okay," she continued. "What did you fight about?"

Mandy felt his body tighten alongside hers. She hadn't thought it possible for him to be any more tense. And his silence wasn't normal, either. At last he spoke.

"You." The word seemed to have been forced from him.

"Me. I see . . ." But she didn't really. She studied the lines of stress on his face, and without even thinking, she squeezed his hand a second time.

He pressed it against his lips and kissed each slender finger. When their eyes met, the troubled look in the depths of his reached out to her in a silent plea, telling her how much he needed to be with her.

"I changed my mind, lady," he whispered. "We'll talk later." His murky green eyes, still locked with hers, warmed to a deeper green as she smiled knowingly. "Make love with me, Mandy." His low voice was itself a spoken caress. He rose, slowly, tugging her to her feet and drawing her into his arms. "Make love with me."

She lay beside him, replete from their physical union. "Beautiful," she murmured, expressing out loud the thoughts running through her mind.

"Perfect," he returned.

A slow, radiant smile spread across her face.

"Proud of yourself?" he questioned in a teasing voice.

She glanced toward him. His warm gaze was fastened on her, his expression curiously different.

"What's wrong?" she asked, puzzled by unfamiliar sensations.

Luke shook his head and gave her a peculiar kind of grin. He sighed, still gazing at her, then shifted his weight to bring her closer. Reaching out one finger, he brushed it ever so lightly across her lips.

Instinctively she nuzzled and licked his flesh.

Luke blinked, surprised. His smile deepened the grooves in his cheeks.

"Yeah, lady, I like the taste of you, too," he said, his voice huskier than normal.

Mandy drew his finger into her mouth and sucked. He groaned his approval.

"You're special, Mandy," he whispered. "Special."

"You, too, MacLaren." She pushed a fallen lock of hair out of the way.

"I care about you," he admitted, staring deep into her aquamarine eyes.

"Confession, Luke?" Measure for measure she returned the intensity of his gaze. "Why?"

"My brother called you a . . . an unpleasant name."

"You argued because he called me a name?" Her voice rose, heavy with curiosity.

"I almost slugged him, Mandy!"

"Really?" She raised her eyebrows in amazement. "What stopped you?"

"Brianna."

"Thank her for me, will you?" she asked. "I'm glad you didn't slug him, Luke. Physical violence ranks up there with drinking."

"Yeah," he acknowledged. "I don't condone it either, but, well . . . he made me mad!"

"And," she observed, "the anger he instigated precipitated a . . . true confession."

"Yeah. Guess it's about time I admitted to both of us . . . this is more than sexual gymnastics." He hugged her closer and brushed her swollen lips tenderly, then captured them beneath his own with surprising force. "Whoever heard of casual sex that was so satisfying, so fulfilling, so beautiful you knew you'd found perfection?"

"Who indeed?" she whispered against the fullness of his lips.

"We made love tonight, Mandy," he informed her seriously. "You admitted it was beautiful."

"I did and it was."

"Lady, I need you. I care about you. What Jess said today made my gut tighten with fury. I felt as if I had to defend your honor, your good name. . . . Oh, sweet angel, it all seems so complicated."

"Why?" she whispered.

"My brother wants to meet you," Luke began.

"The same brother who called me a name?"

"Yeah, the same," he acknowledged. "He asked me to bring you home to meet the clan. I refused." Luke paused, remembering the harsh exchange with his older brother. "You see, lady, I'm not sure I'm ready to share you with all of them. I, well, I'm happy with us, with our relationship, the way we are," he tried to explain.

"And?" she prompted.

"And . . . if I take you home, it'll change our relationship. But if I don't, then my brother will assume it's because I'm ashamed of you."

Mandy tilted her head to stare at him. "How do you think our relationship would change?"

"Consider, Mandy mine, how I'm expected to introduce the woman whose bed I share each night?"

"You could try telling them I'm your friend, Luke," she suggested.

"You are my friend," he insisted. "There's a complication here. My brother and his wife have been staying at my parents' house since the funeral. Jess commented on my nocturnal absence. My parents have, no doubt, observed my absence, also. Do you follow my line of thinking?"

She sighed. "I do."

"How would you feel, friend?"

"I might be embarrassed initially," she confessed. "But I'm not ashamed of our relationship."

"Me neither," he told her. "As a matter of fact, I think I'd like to alter the status quo—with your approval, of course."

"Alter?" she queried, just a touch of trepidation in her husky voice.

"No need to panic, Mandy. Your *lover*—" he em-

phasized the word "—is not about to abandon you."
Luke hesitated, running his hand adoringly through her
soft hair.

"I had a long talk with Sara today. She reminded
me that life is short and unpredictable. I'd like to think
I haven't wasted too much of mine. I want to make the
most of what I have left." He made a face, rolling his
eyes toward the heavens.

"You know, sometimes I have a problem expressing
myself. What I'm trying to ask you, Mandy, is, well,
how would you feel about sharing this apartment?"

"Living together?"

"Yeah."

Mandy pretended to be thoughtful. She purposely
made him wait for her response. He'd actually seemed
hesitant to put the idea into words—after what they had
shared!

"So," she proclaimed, "MacLaren the gigolo."

Luke broke into a relieved grin, then laughed outright. "If you behave yourself, lady," he informed her
playfully, "I'll consider splitting expenses and work
detail fifty-fifty."

"I'll give it some thought," she said. "I'll have to
consider how I'll benefit from this . . . arrangement."

"Mandy . . ." Luke threatened lightly.

She risked a hasty glance in his direction and witnessed his sea-green orbs darkening with emotion.

"Okay," she relented. "I'd like to share my apartment with you, Luke."

"Would you rather look for something else? I'm on
pretty good terms with this Realtor."

"No," she told him. "I'm comfortable here. And
I'd venture a guess that my *lover* is more than capable
of making himself right at home. If we moved," she
added, "we'd never pull off the impromptu midnight

snacks. It'd take hours to find the tray, the coffee carafe, and the—''

"Okay!" he halted her, placing both hands in front of himself as if to ward off attack. "I'm convinced. We stay here."

"Terrific!" she proclaimed. "Glad you saw it my way. We may, um, have to make adjustments . . . living with each other. It's probably best not to move."

"Yeah," he agreed. "So when do we make the change? Tomorrow too soon?"

"Tomorrow is fine."

"Mandy?" His voice was husky with emotion. "Do you want to meet my family?"

She swallowed the sudden lump in her throat. "I think I'd like that, Luke, but I'm not sure I'm ready."

"Maybe we can take it slow. Get together with Jess and Brianna some evening," he suggested, watching for her reaction.

"It's your decision, Luke."

"No, sweet angel," he corrected softly. "This ought to be a joint decision. Don't you think living together implies sharing?"

Mandy nodded in agreement. "You're right, it does," she conceded. "I'd very much like to share those kinds of decisions with you."

"Only those kinds?" he teased.

"Listen, MacLaren, you like the lingerie I choose, you like the food I cook—''

"Which you may have overcooked in this case," he commented.

"Omigosh! Our dinner!"

"Forget dinner," he ordered calmly. "Concentrate on our decisions."

"Luke MacLaren, you're bordering on being incorrigible again. I need to check the moussaka."

"Yeah, right," he agreed. "And, Mandy, you can

decide on lingerie and meals without my input. I'll be in perfect agreement with you. Except," he added, "except if you make Brussels sprouts or rutabagas, in which case, I will unconditionally refuse to eat!"

Mandy laughed. "I can see we're going to be making some compromises."

"You like Brussels sprouts?"

"No, actually, I detest Brussels sprouts. My brother Ben loved them sprinkled with parmesan cheese."

"Yech!"

She laughed again. "Clothe your cute buns, MacLaren. I'll need your help with the salad. You don't want the cook to be distracted after she's come this close to ruining your dinner."

"Long as I get my dessert," he mumbled.

A knowing gleam danced in her eyes. "Don't you always?"

"Yeah," he drawled with obvious delight.

Luke moved his clothes into Mandy's apartment the following morning. She made space in her closet and her dresser drawers for his things. Smiling to herself, she helped him unpack, lovingly placing his very sexy bikini briefs next to her ultrafeminine lingerie.

The room was quiet, she realized, too quiet. She spun around and found Luke standing motionless next to the closet, watching her.

"What's wrong now?" she asked.

"Happy?"

"Yes, I'm happy."

"Good," he said. "Come here and kiss me good-bye."

"You're leaving? You've just unpacked."

"Yeah, well . . . I'd like to move a few of my most treasured possessions, but I think perhaps, I need to tell my family."

"Oh," she responded solemnly.

"Right," he acknowledged. "Ohhh!"

"Will they understand?"

"Yes, I think they will," he said. "Do I get a good-bye kiss, lady?"

She crossed the room and wrapped her arms around his neck. "One for luck," she informed him. "And one for the road, and one—"

"Ummm," Luke silenced her with his hungry mouth.

He left for home an hour later, after they'd made love and shared one final good-bye kiss.

Luke strolled into the kitchen and automatically opened the refrigerator door. He was foraging. It was a MacLaren pastime.

"Hi, Mom," he called over his shoulder. "Dad is expected for lunch, isn't he?"

"He said he'd be late," she explained. "He should be here in about half an hour. Sara and Brianna fed the children. Rachel went to the library. She won't be back for lunch. Ethan disappeared early, but I suspect he'll come from the yard with your father."

"Ahh," he commented. "A quiet adult luncheon."

"We don't have many quiet times, do we?"

"No, Mom," he said, "and you love the noise, don't you?"

"I can't say I love the noise. But I do love all of you and I love having you here. Most of the time the noise doesn't bother me."

"How would you feel if we weren't all here?"

"You aren't all here," she returned. "Drew's gone. Are you trying to tell me you're moving out, Luke?"

"Yeah, but I'm not going far," he said. "Just into an apartment. I'll be back frequently. Promise."

"I guess I'm not surprised," she revealed after a

moment. "You've been gone more than you've been here lately. I suppose that's as it should be. Most men your age are out on their own. . . . I'll miss you, honey."

"No tears, Mom," he begged. "I'll be as close as the phone. If you need me, I'm here."

"I know. But I'll worry just the same. You're a lousy cook, Luke."

"Don't let Brianna hear you say that," he began.

"Sure, you've come a long way, but—"

"Don't worry, Mom," he emphasized. "I won't be cooking for myself. My . . . roommate will prepare our meals. I'll set the table, wash the dishes. Delegation of responsibilities, you know."

"Your roommate," his mother repeated, studying her second son as he helped himself to a large bunch of grapes and began popping them in his mouth one at a time.

"Yeah . . ." He hesitated. "I wanted to talk to you and Dad together." His tone was unusually subdued.

"A woman, Luke?" she questioned perceptively.

He nodded. "A *special* woman."

"I'm not surprised," she stated again, focusing on the shredded carrots in front of her instead of her son.

"I didn't think you would be. I hoped you wouldn't be . . . disappointed or disapproving."

"It's your decision."

She didn't sound judgmental. Neither of his parents would. Yet he knew both of them wanted and expected each of their children to choose traditional lifestyles.

"Mom, I know you would prefer—"

"Luke," she interrupted, "no one expects you to do what we would prefer. You make your own decisions. We trust you to choose wisely."

"Yeah," he mumbled, scratching his head.

The back door slammed. A dark-haired ball of energy

suddenly hit Luke with a body block. "Uncle Luke!" Noah yelled. "Mom and Aunt Sara took us to the park. It was great. I climbed to the way tippy-top of the jungle gym. Aunt Sara made me get down. But it was great!"

Luke laughed and lifted the child onto his shoulders. "Way tippy-top, huh? Bet your mom loved that."

"Sara said I was turning white with fright," Brianna revealed as she wrapped her arms around him and squeezed.

"You look okay now, pretty lady," he pronounced, returning her hug.

"How about me, dear fellow?" Sara interjected coyly. She spun around and struck a model pose, looking absolutely born to the role. "How do I look?"

He released Brianna abruptly. "Hold on, Noah!" he commanded as he grabbed his sister and drew her into his arms like a lover.

"You, my auburn-haired vixen," he declared, "are as lovely, as enticing—"

The back door slammed again muffling the words.

"As desirable as ever I have seen you," he finished, his voice low and sensual as he pulled his sister closer.

"Call the doctor, Mom," Ethan instructed. "Looks like Luke's flipped out. He's saying sweet things to his sister!"

Everyone laughed. Noah clung to his uncle's shoulders as Sara and Luke embraced.

"Good to see that old sparkle of devilment in your eyes, Luke," his father commented as he and Ethan joined the others.

Sara tickled Luke's ribs.

"Hey, witch! Cut that out!" Luke ordered. "If I drop Noah, big brother will be furious. I'm in enough trouble here. Why don't you— Stop, Sara!" he repeated. "Go do something useful and womanly, like put the little darlings to bed."

"Luke MacLaren," she threatened, "if you weren't holding our brother's only son, I'd get you for that! Why don't you try to do something useful yourself!"

"I'll help Mom set the table," he offered. "Time to get down, sport," he told Noah, gently placing the boy on his feet. "Grandma's gonna want me to practice my kitchen skills."

"Lord knows he needs the practice," came a voice behind him.

"Why you little—" He grabbed at Brianna as he spoke, swinging her into his arms and over his shoulder. "I ought to—"

"You ought to put my wife down before you drop her." Jess's words surprised him. No one had heard him enter above the noise and laughter of their shenanigans.

"Yeah," Luke agreed. "She was right. I need practice."

"Practice?" Jess queried. "I believe I missed something crucial here." He took his daughter from her grandmother's arms and bent to hug his son.

"Table setting," Luke grumbled playfully.

"Last time I noticed, fast-food chains weren't requiring their patrons to be well versed in the fine art of table setting."

"That was before salads, Jess," Jonas MacLaren informed him, more than a hint of jest in his deep voice.

"Of course," Jess allowed. "However, Dad, you are forgetting that Luke prefers burgers and fries . . . always has."

"I'll have you know, I make terrific salads," Luke defended. "Edible, too."

"Since when?" Jess challenged.

"I'd like an answer to that," Brianna said. "Last

time I asked you to slice tomatoes, you pulverized them.''

"I've practiced," Luke informed her. "Actually, I'm better at tomato wedges than slices."

"And you know the difference?" she teased. "I'm impressed."

"Interesting," Jess remarked.

"I think I'll put Bethany down for a nap," Brianna announced, tactfully changing the focus of everyone's attention. "That way we can eat lunch without too much distraction." She grasped the child from her husband's arms, gave him a quick little kiss, and with her customary gracefulness, exited the kitchen.

Only the men and Mrs. MacLaren remained. Sara had unobtrusively removed her two small daughters a few minutes earlier.

"Ethan. You and I ought to wash," Jonas suggested. "How much longer, Libby?" he asked his wife.

"No more than ten minutes," she responded. "Much less if these two scalawags help." There was a merry twinkle in her eyes as she glanced at her sons.

She turned back to the carrots, smiling to herself. They were alike in many ways. Their faces, their expressions, were so similar, they almost seemed cloned, except for Luke's mustache. Yet each was his own man. Jess, standing there, hands in his pockets, jingling his coins, dressed in an oh-so-proper business suit, looking like the serious Boston lawyer he was. Every hair on his auburn head was combed neatly in place. Luke, in his faded jeans and worn flannel shirt, thumbs tucked into his belt loops, chestnut hair waved and tousled, worn-looking Reeboks on his sockless feet. But she'd seen the storm warnings clouding their hazel eyes.

The silverware jangled behind her and she realized that while she'd been wrapped in her motherly musing, her sons had sprung into action. Jess was rattling plates. Luke was counting out forks.

"I believe I owe you an apology," Jess said in a quiet voice.

"No, you don't," Luke contradicted. "An apology is in order, but it's not me you offended."

"You realize I didn't mean what I said?"

"Yeah," he smiled. "I figured it out, counselor. You were baiting me. You always have, probably always will. Thanks. I believe your intention was to make me open my eyes wider?"

"In a manner of speaking."

"It worked. As I told Mom a short while ago, I'm moving out."

With a surprising thud, Jess set the plates on the table. "You're what?"

"He's found a roommate," Libby MacLaren intervened.

Jess ran his fingers through his hair. His mother noticed the suit coat was gone and his shirt buttons opened. He looked younger, more relaxed like this, and she smiled once more at the puzzled expression he wore.

"A roommate," he repeated.

"Yeah."

"A roommate?" Jonas MacLaren echoed. He was barely through the doorway. "Luke?"

"I'm moving out, Dad." Luke explained, with a slight shrug.

"Male or female?" Jess interrogated.

Luke shot him a look that spoke volumes.

"Female," their father guessed. "Am I right?"

"Right," Luke admitted.

Jess shook his head in confusion. "I don't believe this," he muttered.

"You might tell us the lady's name," Jonas prompted.

"That would be nice," his wife commented matter-of-factly.

"Her name is Amanda Burke," Luke said. "She's—"

"The realtor?' his mother interrupted.

Luke grinned, then nodded in affirmation. "You've obviously seen the Burke and Benson signs."

"It's hard to miss the one on the next block, Luke. When are you moving out?"

Luke's gaze flicked from his mother to his father. "I moved my clothes this morning," he revealed. "I'd hoped to move a few pieces of furniture this afternoon."

Breaking his long silence, Jess asked, "Need help? I'm free after three-thirty."

"Thanks. I just might need an extra pair of hands."

Ethan and Sara entered the kitchen together, laughing over the children's nap-time routine.

"Brianna's having trouble getting Bethany settled. She said we should start without her," Sara informed them.

"I think we interrupted some high-level discussion, sis," Ethan quipped. "An eerie silence pervaded the room as they entered," he intoned.

"Goose!" Sara scolded.

"Goose!" he shot back. "But I'm right." He swung around, leveling his pointed finger at each of them. "Just look at those guilty faces."

Even Jess was amused by the antics of his youngest brother. "Freckles, the detective," he muttered.

"Listen, big brother," Ethan threatened playfully, "one of these days I'm gonna deck you for calling me Freckles!"

"Sure you are," Jess returned. "You've been telling me that for years."

"You need reminding," Ethan responded. "Drew is the one with two billion freckles!"

"I stand corrected," he returned.

"So, who's the victim?" Ethan inquired, swaggering cockily toward the dinner table. "And what sinister subject are you trying not to discuss in front of an innocent youth such as I?"

"How did you and Dad manage to raise such a smart aleck?" Sara asked, shaking her head. "He's incorrigible!"

Unexpectedly Luke broke out in laughter. The family stared at him, until, at last, he stood there quietly, wearing a silly smile.

"I didn't intend to be quite so humorous," Sara said.

"I know," Luke informed her with a twinkle in his eye. "Just amused me."

"Why is it that everyone is ignoring my inquiry?" Ethan tried again.

"Because you are an impressionable youth and no one wants to inform you of the wicked deeds of your older siblings," Luke stated, his eyebrows raised à la Groucho Marx, as he fingered his mustache in a villainous gesture.

"Yeah, right," Ethan returned. "What was it that you did, oh wicked, shameful sibling?"

"Nothing much. Only decided to cut the apron strings and move out of the old homestead." Luke attempted to treat the subject lightly. He shrugged at Ethan.

"I don't buy it," Ethan told him. "Not wicked and shameful enough."

Jess chuckled. "Smart-aleck kid."

"Where are you going to live?" Sara directed her attention to Luke as she pulled out a chair to sit at the table.

"An apartment about twenty minutes from here," he said somewhat evasively. "I won't be far, Sara. And I won't be a stranger. I promise. You're still my family.''

Luke felt his elder brother's eyes upon him.

"Family first. Right, big brother?'' he challenged.

Jess didn't smile, and the nod he gave was almost imperceptible, yet Luke knew his comment had been acknowledged. He knew, too, that Jess hadn't entirely accepted his decision to leave the fold.

"Why is everyone so quiet?'' Brianna asked in her soft voice as she took her place beside Jess at the table. "This is not a typical MacLaren gathering.'' She glanced at her husband and, following his eyes, realized he was staring at his brother. She placed her napkin on her lap and touched Jess's arm lightly with her fingertips. "You two haven't started arguing again, have you?''

Jess shook his head. "No. Luke gave our *discussion* some consideration. He's decided to live with his lady.''

"Hot dog!'' Ethan yelled. "I knew something wicked was in the works!''

"Incorrigible,'' Sara muttered.

"Ethan!'' Libby MacGregor scolded.

Jess chuckled. Brianna grinned. Luke looked uncomfortable. "I think 'wicked' is a poor choice of words, Ethan,'' he said.

"Your words,'' Ethan returned.

"Yeah, but I never have had a way with words. Big brother's the eloquent one.''

"You're really gonna live with your lady?''

"I am,'' Luke admitted.

"When can we meet her?'' Sara asked curiously.

Luke didn't answer. He was distracted when Jess suddenly rose from his chair and moved toward the small boy standing in the doorway.

"What's wrong, Noah?''

The boy sniffed and rubbed his eyes with his fist. "I heard you talking. Is Uncle Luke going far away like Uncle Drew?"

"Let me handle this, Jess," Luke suggested, pushing himself away from the table. "Hey, sport, I wouldn't leave my favorite nephew." He crouched in front of Noah. "Who else would go fishing with me?"

"But you're moving," Noah argued.

"Just a couple of blocks away. I'll be closer than Aunt Sara is," he explained. "Come on, dry your eyes, and I'll read you a story. How about a fishing story?" he asked as he hoisted the child to his shoulders and left the kitchen.

EIGHT

By four o'clock, Luke and Jess had loaded a few treasured possessions onto a small pickup truck emblazoned with the clipper logo of MacLaren Shipbuilders. Jess drove the truck while Luke led the way in his car. Fortunately the parking lot at Mandy's apartment building was not crowded. They parked near the front door and got straight to the task of unloading and carrying Luke's meager possessions to the third floor.

No more than two steps inside the front door, Jess paused unexpectedly, hanging on to an old rocking chair without thought to the weight or bulk of his load.

"Are you gonna drop what you're carrying by the door or are you going to come in?" Luke asked.

"I stopped to smell the flowers," was Jess's retort.

Luke shot his brother an odd look.

"This isn't how I pictured you living," Jess explained. "This is formal. Structured. You aren't."

"Yeah. This isn't Mandy, either. This is left over from her marriage."

"She's married?"

"Divorced."

"Divorced. Great."

"She had a lousy marriage," Luke was quick to point out.

"All right. I can accept that," he allowed. "I'm accustomed to hearing about lousy marriages."

"That brings up another problem," Luke began. "Your firm handled the divorce. She's uncomfortable with that knowledge."

"I wasn't her lawyer," Jess said.

"James was."

"No problem."

"Yeah, I know that, and you know that, but—"

"When you get around to introducing us, I promise to assure her that any confidentiality is still intact."

"Thanks." Luke grinned, grateful his brother understood.

"Where do you want this old rocker?"

"In the bedroom. This way," he indicated with a crook of his head.

Jess followed. He took one step into the bedroom and froze for the second time. A low whistle escaped him.

Luke laughed. "This is Mandy," he proclaimed.

"Likes satin and lace?" Jess queried.

Luke cleared is throat. "Yeah, she does. That's obvious. I like it, too," he admitted, his grin widening.

"Long as she's wearing it?" Jess mused.

"Satin's not bad to sleep on," Luke replied.

Jess gave him a peculiar look.

"Our bed has satin sheets," Luke explained.

"I gathered as much from your comments," he remarked. "I told Drew the lady had class."

"Drew? What—"

"She was the one we saw with you at The Pub, wasn't she?"

Luke thought for a moment, then answered, "Yeah,

Mandy came looking for me. I'd stormed out of her apartment insisting I needed a drink. I cooled down minutes after I left her, but she didn't know that," he shrugged.

"You never stay angry for long."

Luke shook his head. "Mandy had reason to be worried. Her father was an alcoholic, and we met at The Pub."

"Fortunately some women stick by us, no matter what."

"Mom, Brianna, Sara . . ." Luke said quietly.

"Saints," Jess declared.

"While we sinners continue to give them every reason—"

"Would you look at this," a husky female voice drawled, "two MacLarens in my bedroom at the same time. Must be my lucky day!"

Mandy stood in the doorway where Jess had been minutes earlier. She was dressed in her usual business suit. This one was navy. The tailored blouse she wore was white. A red scarf knotted at her neck served as a tie.

She glanced at Jess, merely acknowledging his presence, then her eyes feasted on Luke in his worn jeans and scruffy Reeboks. His faded shirt, sleeves rolled to his elbows, was opened almost to the waist, revealing the broad, muscular chest with which she was so familiar. She stared with a kind of fascination, feeling a new and different pleasure sweeping through her.

"Mandy," Luke rasped, as the initial shock of surprise left him. "This is my brother, Jess."

She tore her gaze from Luke, politely extending her slender hand toward his brother. "I'm pleased to meet you, Jess."

He took her hand in his and held it, smiling warmly.

"I'm pleased to meet you, too, Mandy and glad Luke finally introduced us."

"And are you the same brother who dared to call me some scandalous name?" she asked spunkily.

Jess swallowed. He had a fleeting glimpse of how it felt to be on the witness stand. Luke and his lady shared quite a bit, it seemed, besides their satin sheets.

"I owe you an apology," he admitted. "I am the brother who so wrongly accused you."

Mandy smiled, eyes dancing merrily. "No apology necessary. You helped bring MacLaren to his senses. I'm grateful for that."

Jess shot Luke a look somewhat akin to amazement.

Luke shrugged his shoulders and looked sheepish. "Clones," he muttered. "Mr. Frank and Ms. Candid."

Without warning, Jess pulled Mandy toward him, giving her a quick, brotherly squeeze. "It seems you and I are going to get along fine, Mandy." As he held on to her longer than necessary, he explained, "I owe him. He is forever hugging my wife."

Grinning capriciously, Mandy returned the hug. "Do you think we'll be able to keep him in line . . . between the two of us?"

"Perhaps. It's hard to say."

"Enough, you two!" Luke proclaimed. "I'm right here in the room while you're talking around me. And I'm beginning to feel neglected. You've got my lady in your arms, big brother."

"Shoe's on the other foot."

"Get over here, Amanda!" Luke ordered.

"Not in front of your brother!" she mocked.

"Hell," he bit out. "Can't I even steal one innocent little 'hi ya' kiss?"

She moved seductively toward Luke, stopping inches in front of him. She slid her hands from his waist across his chest, then wound her arms around his neck, urging his head forward till their foreheads touched.

"Hi ya," she whispered.

"If you two want to be alone—" Jess began.

"Oh, no," Mandy responded. "I'm not that much of an animal. I can stop after an innocent kiss. Luke, however, is another matter entirely. He seldom makes it to the—"

"Amanda!" Luke gasped, swiftly silencing her with his mouth.

Jess departed, leaving them locked in a sizzling embrace. He was amused, and at the same time relieved. Luke's lady was perfect for him. Exactly what Luke MacLaren needed. Jess was immeasurably pleased.

When he ventured back into the apartment carrying a heavy carton of books, he met Luke on his way out.

"Don't forget you were going to pass on some of your MacLaren assurance, counselor," Luke reminded him.

"Immediately," he responded, nodding.

From the kitchen, Mandy called out, "Lemonade, Jess?"

"Please," he answered, placing the heavy carton on the floor in the hallway. He returned to the kitchen, clearing his throat as he approached Amanda.

"Oh, no," she wisecracked. "Luke's out of earshot and you're going to hit me with a brotherly lecture."

"Wrong," he intoned. "I have instructions to assure you that anything you told our cousin James in confidence will remain that way."

"Ohhh. You are blunt."

"Luke indicated you were reluctant to meet me. I wanted to allay your fears as quickly as possible."

"I appreciate that," she said quietly. "My divorce was quite nasty. I haven't discussed the sordid details with Luke, and I wouldn't want him to hear them from anyone else." She sighed heavily. "It's that simple. I have to trust you because I have no choice. I'm not ready to burden Luke with cold, brutal divorce stories."

"I'm not sure he's ready to experience cold, brutal tales of divorce at this stage of his life. He's recently come through—"

"His own personal hell," she finished for him. "I know. He doesn't need to hear my version."

"You're all right," Jess decided.

"Thanks. I like you, too."

Luke entered the room and dumped another carton of books on the counter. He eyed Mandy and his brother suspiciously. "Okay, lady, spill your guts," he ordered.

"I like your brother, MacLaren." She didn't look up at either of them, just concentrated on her task of pouring lemonade into tall glasses.

"To whom are you speaking, Mandy mine?" Luke inquired in a mock-threatening tone. He strode to her side, possessively placed his arm on her waist, and drew her against his muscular frame.

"Makes a difference, does it?" she teased.

"Yeah, it makes a difference," he admitted. "I'm gonna make you pay for this."

Mandy turned and melted into his embrace. "Later," she murmured, "when we're all alone. I promise I'll pay." She winked at him. "Your lemonade is ready."

"And so am I," Luke whispered in her ear.

"Later," she promised, waltzing out of his arms.

"Truck's almost empty, isn't it?" Jess asked.

"One more trip ought to do it." Luke watched as Mandy moved out of sight. "Thanks for your help."

"No thanks are necessary." He shrugged his broad shoulders. "What are families for, if not to help one another when needed. I'm glad I offered. Besides, I finally got to meet your beautiful friend," he remarked.

"You were right, by the way, she is very beautiful. Drew thought so, too, but then, he always was drawn to leggy blondes. Curious, isn't it? In the past you've shown a marked preference for brunettes."

"Curious," Luke repeated. "As I recall, Drew isn't the only MacLaren who often wore a blonde on his arm."

"Touché," Jess responded. "You seem happy with your blonde and I am enchanted with my lovely dark-haired lady." He grinned, then gave Luke a thumbs-up signal. "I approve . . . as if it matters."

"It does, you know. Somehow it does matter," Luke revealed quietly as the two men descended the stairs to return to the truck for the last of Luke's treasures.

The following Thursday evening Luke stood in the doorway of their bedroom, wrapped in a bath towel, still dripping from his shower. He and Amanda had accepted a dinner invitation from Jess and Brianna. It was a big step, sharing Mandy with his family. And yet, when he thought about it, he realized he was ready to take this step, confident he was doing the right thing for everyone concerned.

Unaware she was being watched, Mandy rummaged through her closet, obviously disturbed by something. Luke saw her pull out first one hanger, then the next, silently rejecting each garment and thrusting the hanger back into place.

After a few minutes' observation, he asked, "What's wrong?"

Not turning to look at him, she heaved a sigh. "I can't decide what to wear." Even her voice sounded agitated.

"I've never seen you experience any difficulty with your wardrobe. You always look great. What's the problem tonight?"

Now she turned to face him. "I want to wear the right thing. I'm nervous about meeting your brother's family," she admitted woefully.

"You've met Jess. Bethany's not quite thirteen months old, so she won't care. Noah's only six. He'll love you 'cause you're with me. That only leaves Brianna, and believe me, if I know Brianna, she's more concerned about meeting you than you are about meeting her!"

"You've always implied she has a positive influence on you and your family. I don't understand why she would be nervous meeting me."

"She has been a good influence," he explained. "But she's a quiet little lady, and until she knows someone well and is comfortable with them, she's very reserved. Jess and I have benefited the most from her calm, quiet strength. She looks delicate, but she can be tough if she has to be. The past two years have brought a lot of changes in her life. She's adapted to being a part of our large, busy family, and we've accepted her as one of our own." Luke smiled, remembering.

"You're getting off easy by comparison, Mandy. Jess brought Brianna home to meet the family one Sunday at dinnertime. She was overwhelmed! I've already announced my intentions to take it slowly with you." He grinned from ear to ear. "No way do you have any reason to be nervous. I'm sure you'll like Brianna."

Mandy leaned her forehead against the door frame. "You may think I have no reason to be nervous, Luke, but the fact remains that I am."

"Wear the blue jumpsuit. You'll be comfortable enough to play with the kids if you like, casual enough to complement me in my cords, and you'll look absolutely stunning."

She raised her head and stared at him, mouth hanging open in astonishment. He didn't normally make com-

ments about her wardrobe, unless, of course, he was
suggesting she remove a bit of tantalizing apparel. She
realized he was watching her, too.

"You know," she said, "your present attire is a tad
too casual for dinner with your brother and his wife.
That plush peach-colored towel doesn't cover as much
as the cords you indicated you are planning to wear."

"You don't like it?" he challenged.

"Oh, I like it," she returned coyly. "Although peach
isn't really your color."

"Okay," he agreed, whipping off the towel. "How's
this?" He came toward her, naked and aroused.

"Luke!" Her eyes widened with surprise. True, she
had been teasing him, but she hadn't expected him to
respond as he did.

"Now, Mandy mine," he commanded huskily, "you
are definitely overdressed for the occasion. Strip!"

"Luke," she repeated breathlessly. "We'll be late!"

"Believe me, lady," he informed her as he swiftly
relieved her of her robe, "my brother will understand
our tardiness." He kissed her eyelids closed, trailed a
line of soft kisses along her cheekbone, and murmured
in her ear, "Besides, you'll be more relaxed—mel-
lowed—after we make love."

He was right, of course. She was sated and mellow,
flushed and glowing in the aftermath of their loving.
The intensity of his feelings, more obvious than usual
as they came together, spoke volumes. She went
through her preparations for the evening calmly and
quietly, as if she'd never had second thoughts at all.
When she was ready she looked stunning, yet somehow
casual, like there hadn't been any effort on her part.

Mandy wore the blue jumpsuit, which matched her
bright eyes perfectly. She chose silver earrings, long
and dangling, and a simple silver choker and wrist-

band. On her feet were low-heeled sandals, the same shade of blue as her outfit.

Luke smiled to himself as he watched her in the kitchen. Jess had requested Luke's best possible attempt at a salad, and Mandy had insisted upon creating clown-faced cupcakes for the children. He studied her intently. Her movements were graceful, elegant, even doing such mundane things as wiping the countertop with a cloth.

"You're beautiful," he whispered.

"I'm ready to leave," she returned saucily.

He held out his hands. "Let's go, gorgeous! I'm hungry!"

"Shouldn't be," she teased. "You've already had your dessert."

Jess greeted them at the door, balancing the baby on his hip and holding a large Irish setter at bay with his foot. "The dog's friendly," he informed Mandy, who held Luke's hand in a death grip. "Please tell me if you have an aversion to animals. I'll be happy to remove her to another room."

"She's beautiful. Let her stay," Mandy told him, smiling.

Jess nodded and reached to take the cupcakes from her hands.

As he turned to place them on a nearby table, a dark-haired flash of lightning streaked by her, bolting into Luke's legs.

"Hi, Uncle Luke!" Noah squealed.

"Hi, sport," Luke chuckled, returning the child's tight squeeze while he juggled the salad. "Noah, this is Mandy. She's a friend of mine."

"Girlfriend?" the boy asked, wide green eyes moving from his uncle to Mandy and back again.

"Yeah." Luke grinned as he passed the salad to his brother. "Girlfriend."

"The kind you kiss?" Noah asked curiously.

Luke tightened his possessive grip on Mandy's hand. "Yeah," he admitted, releasing Noah, then tousling the child's thick, dark hair. Turning to Mandy, he explained, "I told him all about girlfriends. But then, it seems Jess had a man-to-man talk with him about girlfriends and kissing."

"I see." Her eyes danced with amusement. "The MacLarens educate their heartbreakers early, do they?"

Jess laughed outright. "We do," he admitted.

The dog wiggled playfully against Mandy.

"Sit, Bridgit," he commanded sternly. The dog obeyed. "Noah, why don't you move out of the way. Let Uncle Luke get in the door before you attack."

"Yeah, sport," Luke scolded in a teasing manner. "Don't pounce on me until I'm on the couch. Where's your mama?"

"Bri's in the kitchen," Jess said. "No doubt creating something especially delightful for us to enjoy. Noah, would you tell Mama—"

The child dashed away, leaving his father in midsentence.

"Happens all the time," Luke informed Mandy. "Noah's quicker than a flash."

"I've noticed," she responded, turning slowly to Jess. "This house is magnificent." Her eyes sparkled appreciatively. "I see dozens of houses each week. Few of them have the dignity and charm of this one."

"I agree," he said. "We searched for several months before we found this. Brianna and I fell in love with it immediately. I'd always wanted a house similar to my parents' home in which to raise my own children. This one definitely meets the requirements."

"Yeah," Luke teased. "Lots of bedrooms."

"Plenty of living space inside," Jess clarified as he

moved toward a large rocker, "and plenty of yard out-side for recreation."

"Bedrooms aren't for recreation?" Luke returned, flashing a knowing look at his older brother.

"You have a bedroom fixation, Luke?" He grinned.

Mandy laughed out loud, then murmured softly, "Yeah." She meant for only Luke to hear, but Jess's eyebrows rose, and he chuckled, too.

Luke gently shoved her onto the sofa. "Yeah," he drawled, "Maybe I do, but big brother has seven bed-rooms upstairs. That's one for each day of the week. What does that tell you?"

"He either expects a great deal of company or is planning a large family," she responded merrily.

"Yeah," Luke acknowledged, a silly grin on his face. "He says he wants a large family. If the truth be known—" he lowered his voice and inclined his head closer to hers—"he likes making babies."

"Who likes making babies?" a soft feminine voice inquired.

Luke looked over his shoulder and grinned at his sister-in-law. "I didn't hear you coming."

"I'm not surprised," she scolded. "You were busy making remarks about someone else."

"Your husband," Luke told her. "Come around here and give me a hug."

Instead, Brianna leaned over the back of the couch. "Introduce me," she whispered.

"Brianna, this is Mandy Burke. Mandy this is Bri-anna," he said with a flourish. "How's that?"

"Eloquent," Jess quipped.

"It's nice to finally meet you," Brianna said warmly. "I'm glad Luke brought you along."

"Thank you for inviting me," Mandy replied. "It's a pleasure meeting you, too. Luke talks about you often."

"Oh, no," Brianna groaned.

"Good things," he insisted. "Only good things. Tell her, Mandy. I don't slander my family."

"Only good things," she assured Brianna, laughing.

"Doesn't slander his family, he says," Jess muttered. "Strange. Only moments ago I had the distinct feeling you were throwing scandalous comments in my direction."

"If the shoe fits—" Luke shrugged his shoulders. "Besides, counselor, my observations are not only valid but based entirely on truths. You're the one who insists on integrity. Can you deny—"

"Enough," Jess commanded. "I admit my guilt. I'd lose if I took you to court. All evidence supports your scandalous accusation."

"Wait," Brianna interrupted. "I came in late and obviously missed something. What exactly are you admitting?"

"Don't ask," Mandy suggested, shaking her head in amusement.

Luke and Jess both laughed conspiratorially. Mandy looked at Brianna. "Are they often like this?"

"Hmm," she returned, nodding. "Afraid so."

"Would you like some help in the kitchen?"

"Yes, thanks, as soon as someone answers me." She scowled playfully at her auburn-haired husband, who at the moment didn't look at all like a serious attorney.

Jess grabbed her arm, tugging her onto his knees. "Should I answer you directly, or can I get even first?" He couldn't hold back his laughter.

"By all means, get even," Brianna suggested. "Otherwise this will continue indefinitely," she told Amanda.

"Great," Jess proclaimed enthusiastically. "It seems as though old Luke here, the same guy who has admitted to me his—shall we say—preference for satin sheets—"

"Jess!" Brianna exclaimed. He laughed harder. Mandy blushed, a rosy hue coloring her pale skin. Luke seemed more amused than embarrassed.

"It's called getting even, babe," Jess explained. "Luke's been telling his lady how much I enjoy making babies."

"Luke!" This time Brianna blushed.

Jess pulled her close and brushed a soft kiss across her forehead. "He's right. We certainly can't deny the obvious." His hand moved to rest possessively upon her abdomen. The gesture could not be misinterpreted.

"Again?" Luke queried.

"Again," Jess proclaimed.

"Terrific. Congratulations," he said. "What'd I tell you, Mandy?" His hazel eyes danced with merriment. He drew her close, pressing her against his muscled chest and looking quite pleased with himself.

Jess cleared his throat. "We weren't planning to share our news with anyone yet," he revealed. "As usual, Luke, you goaded me into action."

"And now I have to pay the price and keep a lid on it, right?"

"We'd appreciate your temporary silence."

"You've got it," Luke promised.

"Thanks."

Brianna wiggled free of her husband's hold and stood next to his chair, her eyes locked with his. "Guess I'd better see about our dinner," she said quietly.

"I'll help," Mandy offered, rising to her feet.

"Mandy," Jess called after them. "I'll give you a tour of the house after dinner. . . That was the original topic, wasn't it?"

"I'd like that," Mandy responded over her shoulder.

Mandy found dinner much more enjoyable than she had imagined. Brianna was an excellent cook. She'd prepared Luke's favorite chicken casserole and baked a flavorful dill bread to accompany it. Luke's salad, prepared proudly by him and served with Mandy's delicious homemade yogurt dressing, was a great success, as well as a surprise to his brother. The meal ended with a light custard pie Brianna served piled high with fresh fruit.

The quality of the food itself was not so unexpected, as Luke had frequently spoken of Brianna's cooking lessons. What Mandy discovered was a delightful flow of conversation and unusual camaraderie between the brothers. She was comfortable joining in their bantering exchanges or adding comments to the few serious topics discussed over the course of the evening. She was fascinated by the interactions of these family members.

Jess, she quickly learned, was more serious, more eloquent, and generally had command of the conversation. But he was not overbearing and, as she'd already learned, had a marvelous sense of humor. Luke, on the other hand, kept interjecting his usual witty comments, yet somehow he exhibited as much depth of character as his older brother. Brianna, she observed, was quiet and soft-spoken, obviously intelligent, and more than capable of holding her own in the midst of the overpowering MacLarens.

All in all, dinner was an event Mandy would never forget. She'd seen a facet of Luke that she knew existed but had not previously witnessed. He had told her about these people and their importance in his life. He'd spoken of the love and respect he had for each of them. But tonight she had watched him. She had witnessed the loving exchanges, the tight squeeze emphasizing a bond between Luke and Noah, the warm embrace he had shared unashamedly with Brianna, and the unusual closeness between the two brothers that was apparent not only in their conversation, but also in the unspoken understanding as they nodded or gestured to each other.

After dinner, Mandy and Brianna began the cleanup as naturally as if they'd been working together for years. Jess and Luke continued their conversation, each keeping an eye out for Bethany and Noah, who played not so quietly on the living room carpet.

Brianna was covering the leftover casserole when Mandy carried the last of the china into the kitchen.

"I've enjoyed myself tonight," Mandy stated, a wistful note in her voice. "Your family is delightful."

"Thank you," Brianna responded. "I'll have to admit I'm proud of each one. You know, I probably shouldn't say this, but I'm glad you've cared about Luke enough to help him through this time. He needed something, more than our love, something . . . special. Because he himself is so special. He stood by me when I needed strong shoulders to hold me up. And now it seems as though you've done the same for him."

"He is special," Mandy agreed. "He feels the same way about you—very brotherly and protective. You have his unconditional love and respect."

"Mmm. He's that kind of person. Once you win a place in his heart . . ." She paused to look straight at Mandy. "Guess you know that by now, don't you? He's more relaxed tonight, more like himself, than I've seen him in months. Has to be your influence."

"I'll take some credit for that," Mandy chuckled. "And yes, I have discovered the caring, considerate man behind the silly-guy mask. It wasn't all that difficult, either. It only takes time to listen and earn his trust."

"It's obvious you've given him the time he needed."

"Perhaps," she agreed. "But this family wields more influence than I ever could."

Brianna stared at the stunning blonde standing in her kitchen, working beside her. She appeared comfortable and self-assured in a potentially awkward situation. But Brianna detected a note of wistfulness in her voice.

Mandy stopped drying the dish she held, aware of the weight of Brianna's stare. She glanced in her direction and caught the odd expression on the other woman's face.

"Did I say something wrong?"

"No," Brianna hastened to assure her. "What you said triggered a memory. The MacLaren family as a unit seems awesome. Until you know each of them. They are merely individuals who are intensely loving, fiercely loyal, and as a unit very strong." She smiled. "I know I'm probably not saying this as well as I could, but . . . don't be jealous of them or of their influence on him—"

"Wait," Mandy interrupted. "I'm not jealous of Luke's family. Not one bit. I am envious, very envious. I never had a family like this. My father—" She stopped short, blinking back the tears that had appeared unexpectedly.

The room was silent except for the silverware Brianna rattled while she washed. Finally Brianna murmured, "We're a pair."

Mandy raised tear-filled eyes to study the dark-haired woman. "What do you mean?"

"Strays," Brianna explained, struggling now with her own tears. "The MacLarens have given me so much love that sometimes I forget. You made me remember. . . . It seems as if Jess and Luke have dragged two homeless strays into the fold."

"I'm sorry," Mandy began.

"No," Brianna insisted. "Don't be sorry for me. I had a wonderful family. A perfectly happy childhood. But I haven't been home for a very long time. The

MacLarens are my family now. I love them all as my own. But I don't think any of them could ever begin to understand what it feels like to be alone. They always have one another, and there are so many of them, someone is always available if you need to grab on to an anchor. How could any member of a family like that ever know what loneliness is? Or isolation? Sometimes, not often anymore, I want so badly for things to be different." She stopped and dried her hands. "You're a listener," she said. "Thank heaven."

Mandy smiled. "Luke's a listener, too."

"So is Jess. But sometimes I need a woman who hears. The family's short on them. Sara's more a talker than a listener. And Rachel *never* stops talking!" she emphasized with a shake of her head. "We may have a great deal in common."

"Two strays who know how to listen well?" Mandy suggested.

"More than that. There's our attraction and devotion to MacLaren men."

"Those are considerations."

"And the fact that I feel comfortable enough to admit what I just did to you."

Mandy nodded. "I suppose I should tell you," she said, "I have those feelings, too. I don't let too many people get close. Yet the night I met Luke, I told him about my father's drinking problem, and now I'm telling you how much I envy this family."

"I don't even tell Jess how much I miss my brothers and my little sister. My older sister, Laura, is my only contact with my family. My older brother got married right before Christmas. I didn't even get an announcement, much less an invitation. And I didn't tell Jess. I assumed he wouldn't understand how much I hurt—" She broke off, tears flowing down her cheeks.

"And Luke thinks the two of you share everything!" Mandy scolded.

"We do, Mandy," Brianna defended. "We've shared everything from the moment we came together again. It's almost second nature. It's not easy to explain, but without Jess it seems as if I'm only half a person. We function together, separate individuals, yet a whole soul, perfectly attuned to each other. Anyway, my family is a finished chapter in a closed book. We don't discuss them. And I've come to the point where I almost never think of them . . . more than once a day." She sighed loudly and long. "It's hard when I'm watching my children or Sara's. I'm sorry, Mandy," she apologized. "I've rambled on and on."

"I was nervous about meeting you tonight," Mandy admitted. "Luke assured me I had no reason to be nervous. He was certain I'd like you." She smiled warmly at the petite dark-haired woman. "He was right. I do like you. I'm glad those overbearing gentlemen have given us this much time alone."

"I am, too," Brianna acknowledged. "Although I don't honestly think they've given any thought to us. They probably started their own reading endurance contest. Basically, it's an example of sibling rivalry at its finest. Noah loves to have stories read to him. That's how the contest begins. Jess reads one. Luke reads one. and so on. As late as it was when they started, Noah more than likely has fallen asleep. And if I know those two men, they're piling up books for the next round."

"Noah and Luke are very close, aren't they?"

She nodded. "Luke spends a lot of time with Noah, and with us, too," she added. "It's part of how the MacLarens view family. You, um, must like children. You made those cute clown-face cupcakes for the kids."

"I like children," she responded quietly.

"I'm not trying to be nosy, Mandy," Brianna explained, "but I noticed an odd expression on your face when Jess revealed my pregnancy. I wondered whether you disapproved or whether you didn't like children."

"Envy. Pure and simple."

"No," Brianna countered. "That fleeting look I saw in your eyes wasn't envy."

"Perceptive," Mandy murmured. "Most of what I was feeling then, and am feeling now, is envy. The look you must have seen—" she hesitated "—that feeling wasn't directed at you or your children, Brianna. Most probably you glimpsed my own . . . private moment of pain." Mandy took a deep breath.

"It was pain," Brianna whispered, realizing now as she watched a sadness cloud Mandy's lovely features. "But, why?"

"I had a miscarriage several years ago." She shook her head. "Secrets. I detest them. I can't bring myself to tell Luke."

"I won't betray your confidence," she assured her. "But you ought to tell him."

"He knows we tried unsuccessfully to have children. I couldn't tell him the truth."

"You should," Brianna urged.

"Well, like you said, Brianna. We're a pair. You ought to tell Jess how you feel about your family. Luke doesn't need to know every detail of my life."

"Yet," Brianna added.

"Yet," Mandy echoed.

"We ought to finish the dishes," Brianna remarked.

"And dry our eyes before we get caught," Mandy suggested, wiping her hand across her tear-streaked face.

"And find something cheerful to discuss."

"Your house!" Mandy proclaimed. "Jess promised me a tour of this magnificent old house."

'Well, then, what's keeping us? Forget the dishes! Let's go.''

They each stopped what they were doing, washed and dried their hands, and had almost made it to the kitchen door when the men appeared in the doorway only a few feet in front of them.

"What's this? A mutiny?" Jess teased. "The scullery maids are escaping before the work is finished.''

"Aha!" Luke quipped. "We caught them just in time! What shall we do with them?"

"Bri, you've been crying. What's wrong?" Jess implored, concern etching his handsome face as he approached his wife. He placed strong hands on her small shoulders and held her close to him, his shrewd eyes searching her features, still fresh with the evidence of her recent distress.

At the same time Luke's hard stare pinned Mandy in her place. She lowered her eyes, refusing to meet his gaze. In one sleek movement he was at her side, lifting her chin with his index finger. A brief glance at her wet lashes, red-tinged nose, and the telltale streaks down her cheeks and he knew.

"Mandy's been crying, too," he bit out. "Damn it, lady. Look at me.''

In response, Mandy shook her head. She hadn't managed to compose herself completely, wasn't ready yet for a confrontation with Luke.

"Mandy," he nearly growled. "What the hell's wrong here?''

"Woman talk," she told him faintly.

"Like hell!"

Mandy sniffed and raised her eyes to meet his stormy green ones. "You know how weepy and sentimental women can be," she hinted.

"You're a lousy liar, Amanda Burke." He wiped a stray tear from her face.

"Why don't we talk later?" she suggested, her eyes pleading with him. "Brianna and I were about to start a tour of the house."

Silence filled the room as he studied her. He shook his head in frustration. "No lies between us, Mandy?" he begged softly.

"Later," she whispered.

"Promise?"

"I promise."

Luke enfolded her in his arms and ran soothing hands up her back. "Kiss me," he commanded, urging her closer.

Willingly Mandy obeyed.

A few feet away Jess and Brianna ended the kiss they had been sharing, but neither made any effort to end the embrace. Jess opened his eyes, glancing toward his brother.

"Blue-eyed enchantresses, both of you," he muttered into Brianna's thick hair. "You both believe you can halt our questions with soft, bewitching kisses and promises."

"Hmm?" Luke's mumbled query was almost indistinct.

"Never mind," Jess replied. "Evasive maneuvers are a female specialty."

"Yeah," Luke acknowledged. "Did you get outmaneuvered, too, big brother?"

Jess nodded affirmation.

"No answers?"

"None."

"Okay," Luke proclaimed, throwing his hands in the air. "We admit defeat. Mandy and Brianna were just about to tour this old house, right?"

"Right," Brianna chimed in.

"Onward," Jess declared. "Let the tour begin."

NINE

Mandy was preoccupied as she unfastened the buttons of her jumpsuit. She stared at the closet door, not seeing it, but reliving the evening she had spent in the company of Luke's family. She was experiencing the warmth and acceptance she had felt all evening.

"Spill it, lady," Luke demanded from behind, startling her out of her reverie.

Mandy whirled around to face him, more than half out of her clothes by this time. Luke thought she looked vulnerable and exposed, not only because of her state of undress, but also because there was a hint of something in her eyes, haunting and painful. She was pale, almost white. Her light blond hair, fair skin, and ivory silk underthings molded together to present a white-on-white ghostly image. Only her aquamarine eyes held any color.

In that moment, he realized his cool, self-possessed lady was stripped of her masks, of her props, and was, figuratively and almost literally, naked before him. He realized, too, that she needed his strength.

As he accepted this knowledge he closed the space

between them. One arm skillfully drew her against his solid frame, supporting her weight. The other arm snaked into the closet, pushing hangers as he spoke.

"Let's get you into your robe," he suggested. "You're cold."

Mandy silently acknowledged that he was right. Her flesh was cold, in spite of the tingling inner warmth she had felt only moments before. And now, facing Luke, an unaccustomed fear gripped her. Fear that the truth he asked of her would drive him away.

She knew him well. They had been together nearly five months, sharing not only nights and days, but secrets of the soul. She knew things about him he would never admit to anyone. Mandy knew the man inside Luke MacLaren.

And that's what scared her.

How would the real Luke feel when she told him the truth? She was sure she didn't want to know. What she wanted was to find some way to postpone the unavoidable, some way to delay this discussion. If only she didn't have to reveal her demons just now. Because just now, she needed Luke with her. Revealing the truth might drive him away. She was not prepared for that, though she was certain of the inevitability.

"Luke," she begged softly, "make love to me." She brushed her lips along the flesh of his neck and, at the same time, pressed her body suggestively against his. "Fill me with your heat. I don't need my robe."

"We need to talk," he responded.

"I need *you*, Luke," she insisted, provocatively sliding her hand over the zipper of his slacks. "Now. Please," she begged. "We'll talk . . . afterward."

He groaned and swiftly relented. Picking her up as if she weighed no more than a child, he carried her the short distance to their bed, deposited her gently on the mattress, then hastily removed his clothing.

He did her bidding, granted her wishes. He made love to her slowly, with agonizing tenderness, filling her with his warmth and undeniable passion. They were one. They soared. Journeyed beyond the edge and higher. Together. United. More than lovers . . .

And when they were replete, when the explosive fireworks ended, the rapture remained. They clung to each other and slept.

"I don't like waking up alone, Mandy," Luke scolded softly as he sauntered into the living room.

"Yeah," she tried to tease, "I know. I'm sorry."

"Maybe you should tell me what this is all about," he suggested, plopping next to her on the couch and placing a surprisingly passionate kiss on her soft, warm lips. "I changed my mind," he murmured. "We can talk later."

"You're aroused!" she observed, surprised because she half expected him to be annoyed.

"I need you now, Mandy mine," he whispered, pulling her onto his lap. "I need your sweetness," he told her, covering her mouth with his. "And I need your softness," he breathed as he cupped her breast and caressed her. "And I need all . . . the rest of you," he pronounced, positioning her masterfully over him and drawing them together.

Mandy was a pliant but willing participant. In the ecstasy that followed, Luke, who often remained silent while they made love, displayed an amazing and unusual competency for the art of conversation. He whispered and coaxed as he kissed and caressed her, forcing her to listen as he spoke.

In spite of her impassioned haze, Mandy realized he was forcing her to think, really think, not merely feel every gesture, forcing her to fully experience what was happening. He was demanding, in his own way, that she share more than her body, demanding she share her most intimate feelings with him, encouraging her to open up to him—not only physically, but emotionally as well. With this realization came another. Luke was openly displaying more than caring. He was loving her, even if he hadn't spoken the exact words, it was obvious in every gesture.

In the aftermath of their heated passionate exchange, Luke clutched Mandy close, holding on to her almost desperately.

"Satisfied?" she inquired as she turned in his arms.

"Yeah . . . Physically my needs have been met." He released his tight hold on her, sighing.

"Oh, Mandy," he groaned, "the caring goes so deep. . . . But caring is not enough. . . . Sex isn't enough." He spoke slowly, pausing for long, thoughtful moments between sentences, searching for the right way to express his concerns.

"Trust me, lady?"

She nodded.

"What we say to each other stays here with us."

"Of course."

He studied her intently. "Why do you continue to avoid this discussion? You know we need to talk. You know I'll listen. Don't I always?"

She nodded again.

"Yeah . . . I listen so well, I can hear those repetitive nonverbal responses," he teased. "I'm concerned about you, Mandy. We've committed ourselves to a relationship, haven't we? I mean, we aren't living together just 'cause the sex is fantastic, are we?"

"No, Luke," she answered, her husky voice barely more than a faint, surprised whisper.

"Yet we've made love twice to avoid talking. And before you get defensive, I admit *I needed . . . I asked* the second time. The point is, we still haven't talked."

He tilted her chin, forcing her to look at him. "Your back's against the wall, Mandy mine. No more postponement. Later is now," he informed her. "Spill it. Why were you crying?"

"I . . . we," she began stammering. "They . . . seem so happy."

"Jess and Brianna *are* happy," he corrected.

"I envy them," she revealed quietly. "Their marriage is everything mine wasn't."

Luke scratched his head. "That's why you were crying?" he asked, obviously perplexed.

"Sort of," she hedged.

"Mandy," he began, his deep voice laced with concern, "will you explain 'sort of?' "

"I . . . You aren't making this easy."

"I'm sitting here holding you in my arms. We just made love—exquisitely. I can't speak for you. How much easier do you suppose I can make it?"

She swallowed hard, then muttered, "Yeah, you made your point."

He couldn't help but see the pained expression cross her face. "Where does it hurt?" he whispered, gathering her even closer. "Tell me where it hurts."

"Inside . . . all over," she relied faintly.

"Why? Surely Brianna didn't say anything?"

"She's very observant. She, um, guessed I was upset."

"And you talked to her when you couldn't talk to me?"

Mandy only nodded.

"What hurts you so much you can't share it with me?" he demanded. "Why tell Brianna and not tell me?"

"You're upset," she accused. "Please don't be. I— I haven't felt comfortable discussing this with you. And, um, Brianna was aware something was bothering me," Mandy lifted her eyes to meet Luke's, silently begging for his understanding.

"Yeah, okay. You were comfortable discussing an issue with Brianna. I can understand that. She's a good listener. She's perceptive. But I don't understand why you're avoiding the subject with me," he said. "Actually, I'm disappointed you haven't broached this subject, whatever it is."

Mandy released a long, shaky breath. "There's been no need to discuss having babies, Luke."

An odd, surprised look crossed his face. "No need? If something is hurting you, Mandy, there is, at least, a reason for us to talk."

"Maybe," she allowed, "but it didn't seem right."

"You want children, don't you?" he queried perceptively.

"Yes . . . I—I do."

He studied her solemn face. "And? What is it you *aren't* saying?"

"We tried," she whispered.

"You and David?"

Mandy nodded.

"You said you had tried unsuccessfully. . . ." Luke hesitated, noticing the pain filling her eyes. "You didn't conceive."

She shook her head. "I did. . . ."

"You did? What happened, Mandy? Tell me," he demanded urgently.

"I . . . lost the baby," she whispered, tears streaming down her face.

"Oh, sweet angel, I'm sorry," Luke murmured, caressing her tenderly. "Did Brianna's announcement tonight bother you?"

"It brought back memories," she admitted. "Brianna apparently noticed the expression on my face as I remembered."

"I hope David was better on that occasion than when you lost your brother."

She took a deep, steadying breath. "He wasn't."

"The bastard," Luke bit out roughly.

"Exactly."

"You should have told me," he scolded gently.

"The subject hasn't come up for discussion, Luke."

"Well, now it has. You'd like to have a family."

"Sure," she replied, trying to sound nonchalant.

"Do I detect a 'but' in your tone?"

"Sometimes, Luke, you are too perceptive."

"Spill it!"

"I'm not sure I can go through that again," she revealed quite honestly.

"You're afraid?"

"Yes . . . I'm afraid.

"If you fall off a horse—"

"I don't ride."

"If you were in a car accident, you'd eventually try to drive again."

"Probably."

"This is no different."

"Yes, it is. Physical injuries heal."

"Jess had emotional injuries, too. Time healed those."

"Maybe."

"Aren't you willing to try?"

"I don't know. I'm not sure."

"I'd like a family."

"I know. It was obvious to me whenever you spoke of your nieces and nephew."

"That's because you know me so well, Mandy mine." He smiled, studying her face with an odd light of curiosity in his hazel eyes. "I wouldn't let you down, you know. I'm not David."

"Luke?" she queried hesitantly and so faintly her husky voice was barely audible.

"Somewhere down the road, sweet angel, this relationship . . . this commitment of ours will, no doubt, lead us into a more permanent . . . arrangement."

"Commitment," she echoed.

"Yeah. We've agreed on a sort of commitment, Mandy, living as we are."

"An unspoken commitment."

"Yeah. I suppose I'm assuming more than I should. But the words didn't seem necessary."

"We've said it all without words," she murmured.

"That's what I thought. An unspoken commitment."

"Right."

"And when I want a family," he ventured, "will you be willing to take the risk?"

"What if I can't, Luke? What then?"

"You mean *if* there are complications?"

"Yes," she whispered faintly.

"Mandy, we'll deal with it then."

"We shouldn't ignore the 'what ifs,' Luke. What if *you* desperately wanted to be a father and *I* couldn't make that happen? What if we tried to start a family and I miscarried again? What would you do, Luke, if I couldn't have your children? What would that do to you? Or to our commitment?"

"Our commitment to each other would be just as strong. It's you, Mandy, that I want to be with. True, I would like children. But *if* we weren't successful making babies, we'd still have each other. That's important. You're important—whether or not you're able to bear children. *You* are what matters to me. In the event our own little family doesn't happen, I'm sure we'll compensate by spoiling all our nieces and nephews."

Mandy smiled—a warm, open, loving smile. Her eyes glowed with admiration. She touched the corner of his mustache with one delicate finger. "You sound as if you mean that."

"I do, lady. I'm not giving you up. Not for all the 'what ifs' you throw at me. When we decide we're ready to make babies, when you agree to take the risk, you can be sure I'll be there with you every step of the way—*whatever* happens."

"Oh, Luke, I love you so much," Mandy cried, tears of joy streaming down her face. "You're some kind of friend."

"Yeah. I'm some kind of lover, too. We're gonna be experts at practicing the art of conception, aren't we?"

"Experts. I'm sure we will be," she agreed, smiling. "You're good for me, Luke MacLaren."

"And you, Mandy mine, have become my lifeline. I live for your love, your sweetness, your caring . . . for you."

"Luke," she murmured as he pulled her into his warm embrace and began to work his magic.

Late Tuesday afternoon when Mandy arrived home from work, she was surprised to find Luke in the apartment.

"What are you doing here?" she queried. "It's too early for you to be home."

"Early for you, too. Only four," he said in return.

"Are you working on something here?" she asked, realizing he was bent over his sketch book.

"Yeah. Come see," he invited, not bothering to look up.

Mandy stood where she was and studied him in silence. At times like this it was hard for her to believe this was the same Luke who came into her apartment each evening and hastened to get out of his clothes and into her bed. The Luke she was watching now was the serious artist, the one she rarely saw but knew existed beneath the casual facade. He almost never did any work at their apartment. The lighting wasn't right. And lighting, he'd informed her from the first, was critical. Only occasionally did he so much as pick up his sketch-book at home, and then it was always for a brief time, to add or alter when an idea was fresh in his mind.

Mandy smiled a satisfied smile. This intent man appeared well-pleased with himself . . . and totally contented.

She ambled slowly toward the table to stand behind him, making a conscious effort not to disturb him while he was engrossed in his work. She leaned over his left shoulder and peeked at the house plans spread before him on the table.

"Like it?" His voice was both quiet and hopeful.

"It's fantastic," she exclaimed breathlessly. "Your client must be extremely wealthy. I can't imagine living in a place like that!"

"Do you like it?" he repeated.

"Of course I like it, Luke. Who wouldn't?"

"Lots of people wouldn't. Too modern for some tastes. Too many angles. Too much wood. Too much glass."

"Don't *you* like it?" Mandy asked, disbelief in her low tones. "How could you design something you dislike?"

"When I design, it's for my clients. Most of them have seen my work and like my style. I've never had to design a house I didn't like. That is, I've never been dissatisfied with the finished product. But that doesn't mean I'd like to live there."

"And this particular dwelling?" Mandy queried. "Are you merely satisfied with the magnificent design or would you be happy living in it?"

"I've been working on this 'dwelling,' as you call

it, for about, oh, five years. This is my dream house, Amanda Burke. My fantasy.''

"Ohhhh . . .'' she murmured, accepting and acknowledging the unspoken fact that he'd designed this place when he had other dreams intact.

"I haven't looked at it in months—almost trashed it awhile back,'' he admitted, finally lifting his eyes to meet hers. "No need to dispose of this particular dream, Mandy mine. Only need someone to share it with. I'm glad you responded enthusiastically. Would have been a low blow to this man's ego to have his lady reject the plans to his castle.''

She smiled at him indulgently.

"We need to find the proper place to construct our home. I drove around for a while this morning. What I need, actually, is a Realtor, someone with access to available parcels of land. . . .''

"I have a friend,'' Mandy teased, "Amy Benson. Perhaps she could give you some help.''

"Amy Benson. Yeah,'' he repeated, feigning thoughtfulness. "I recall the name. Burke and Benson Realty. Met the partner—the lovely Amanda Burke—some months ago. I'd rather deal with her.''

"I'm sure we can work out an arrangement, Mr. MacLaren,'' Mandy replied.

"Good,'' he said. "You busy tomorrow morning?''

"No, my schedule tomorrow is lighter than usual.''

"Perfect. Want to join me in my search for the best possible place to build my dream house?''

"I'd love to join you,'' she responded brightly.

"That's settled. How about dinner?''

"I stopped at the butcher's and got those thick pork chops you like. Thought I'd stuff them with—''

"Let's go out,'' he interrupted. "We'll have the chops tomorrow.''

"Out?'' she echoed.

"Yeah, out. To a fancy restaurant," he explained. "I feel like celebrating. Just you and me."

"Okay, I'll put the chops in the refrigerator and we'll go out."

"What's wrong?"

"In the past two weeks we've gone out for breakfast three times, lunch twice, and dinner three times," she tallied.

"And you think that's odd because we never used to go anywhere?" he guessed.

"Right."

"Don't you want to go out with me?" Luke appeared as puzzled and disappointed as a small child whose ice cream has fallen from the cone.

"Of course I do!" she protested.

"That's the way I feel, too, Mandy mine. I want to take you places. I don't know if I can explain, but I'll try." He cleared his throat. "Way back when, I picked up this beautiful gal in a bar and took her home to bed," he began. "I didn't have much desire for bright lights and public places. I needed a place to hide away . . . to crawl into and lick my wounds, I guess. Now I have a mutually satisfying relationship with my lovely lady. No need to hide from the world. As a matter of fact, there's every reason to go out and celebrate. My lady loves me, accepts me as I am, and I've just recently discovered she loves my dream house—our dream house?"

"Our dream house," she repeated huskily.

"Reason enough to celebrate in public, lovely lady?"

"Reason enough," she agreed.

"Reason enough to celebrate in private later?"

"We don't need a reason to celebrate in private, Luke."

"Yeah, right. We never did need a reason for that, sweet angel."

* * *

Mandy sat at her desk the next morning thinking about Luke. The office was quiet. She didn't have any appointments on her schedule except for Luke, and the paperwork in front of her could wait while she savored the memory of the previous evening.

It had been lovely. The elegant restaurant had served delicious food. She and Luke had laughed together, enjoying themselves almost like children playing. Afterward they made love. A perfectly perfect evening. Mandy felt happy, almost bubbly inside. Her life had never brought her such joy and contentment before. Some days she could hardly believe it wasn't all a beautiful, blissful dream.

She was not only remembering last night but that first night, almost six months earlier, when she'd brought Luke home to her bed. What an outrageous whim! She had wanted to know the handsome stranger. Well, she knew him now. And she loved him. Dear Luke. She was sure he loved her, too, even if he couldn't bring himself to say the words. She knew it was unspoken in every caress when they made love, and more than obvious when he made plans for their future together. He didn't act much like that guy who was afraid of being hurt by love, but then, her outlook was different now, too.

She had jumped into this relationship feet first, eyes wide open. Neither of them had intended to fall in love; in fact, they both insisted it had to be casual, no strings. What had happened to their intentions? Somewhere along the way they had become good friends, close friends, loving friends. Slowly, imperceptibly, they'd begun to love with an intensity surpassing their physical desires. Somehow casual sex had become making love, no strings had become iron emotional bonds, just for today had become forever.

Mandy smiled to herself and sighed deeply.

There were still bits of information she hadn't shared with Luke, but she knew sooner or later she'd tell him. She'd have to tell him. David's brutal betrayal of her rang in her ears: "You're not even woman enough to perform a natural task, it seems. I want a whole woman, Amanda, not merely one who looks good, but one who functions as a wife is meant to function. You're pretty, but damn worthless to me. I'll have my lawyer contact you."

Tears trickled down Mandy's face. Luke had assured her he wouldn't react in the same manner, but how could she be sure? And how would she find the courage to tell him she still had one tiny spark of doubt. It wouldn't be easy, but she'd have to find a way.

Luke listened. Luke shared. Luke dreamed. They had shared and dreamed together. That magnificent house he had designed—he wanted to share it with her. She wanted that dream, too, and more. She wanted it all with Luke. And she realized, she especially wanted to hear the words he hadn't offered. Mandy had been patient. Six months she'd devoted to him. She loved him. She could be patient longer. She would wait.

In the meantime, there was the little matter of the paperwork waiting for her. Amanda Burke picked up her pen and resumed working.

"Which of the six lots did you like best?" Luke asked as he stretched out on the living room sofa.

Mandy set her purse on the end table and moved into the kitchen. "You prefer the two overlooking the water, don't you?"

"Yeah, but I'm asking for *your* input, Mandy."

"It's *your* dream house, Luke."

"Yeah. All right. But my dream house will not be complete without the perfect lady by my side. Now, listen up. A house is not a home *unless* there is love inside it. Love, not loneliness. I need you, Mandy, to fill the house with love, to make it a home. And I want to share this decision with you. Which lot did you like the best?''

"The one overlooking the bay.''

"Great!'' he exclaimed. "You're being completely honest, aren't you? You aren't just agreeing on that particular lot because I like the water?''

"Luke, aren't I always truthful?''

"Yeah, except for the sins of omission,'' he accused. "You might say, 'Oh, Luke, I like that one the best,' and what you don't say is, 'except for the one with the big oak trees.' ''

"I am not a devious person!'' she insisted.

"No, you aren't. It's just that this is important. It means—''

"I know. It means everything to you.'' She shook her head and rolled her eyes. Sometimes he was impossible. "We like the same lot, Luke. Honest!''

"Yeah?''

Mandy laughed. "Luke MacLaren, you can say 'yeah' more expressively than any other human being alive. You must have perfected three or four dozen different ways, complete with variable meanings. You amaze me!''

"Yeah?'' he queried, eyebrows raised.

"Yeah!'' she laughed.

"Oh, yeah,'' he teased.

"Enough,'' she scolded.

"Yeah,'' he pronounced decisively. "Enough.''

TEN

As Brianna opened her front door, Mandy greeted her with an apologetic, "Hope you don't mind an early guest. My last appointment canceled. I thought you might be able to use an extra pair of hands before dinner."

"What a wonderful surprise! Come in!" Brianna exclaimed, nudging the dog aside with her foot. "Actually, everything is in order. The table's set. The veal roast is in the oven. Dessert's in the freezer. I baked bread this morning. Mom and Dad are bringing the rest of the meal, and the children are still napping."

"Luke promised a salad, didn't he?" Mandy stepped into the spacious foyer, glancing over her shoulder at Brianna as she spoke.

"He did. Aren't you supervising?"

"No. I was supposed to have a long day. We agreed to meet here," she explained. "I think he can manage the basics on his own."

"Is something wrong?" Brianna placed a caring hand on Mandy's arm.

"I'm a little apprehensive about this dinner, but other than that, nothing's wrong."

"You're sure?"

"Yes," she returned, nodding slowly. "If you were busy, Brianna, I can come back at six when you expect me."

"Silly," Brianna scolded. "I'll put on water for tea and we'll sit in the living room and have a woman-to-woman chat before the family descends on us. Come on." She gestured toward the kitchen. "I'm glad you're early and alone. I was thinking about drawing you aside this evening to beg a favor." Brianna sounded hesitant. "Would you mind watching Noah and Bethany Tuesday morning? I need to make a trip to the obstetrician and I, um, didn't want to answer a barrage of questions from well-meaning relatives."

Mandy watched her fill the teakettle with water. "Problem?"

"Minor. I'll feel better after I discuss it with my doctor," she stated casually. "Would you mind?"

"I don't mind at all. I'd like the opportunity to spend time with your children, but they don't know me very well. Will that be a problem?"

Brianna set the kettle on the burner. "I doubt it. Noah thinks Uncle Luke's girlfriend is gorgeous. Guess he inherited his father's attraction to blondes."

"Blondes?"

"My predecessor was a coolly elegant blonde." She reached for the teacups, seeming intent on placing them on the saucers.

"Ohhhh . . ." Mandy chuckled.

"Go ahead and laugh, but Luke's got a blonde. And I've heard Drew is drawn to them as well, although he never brings anyone home, so I don't have proof."

"I must be a shoo-in," Mandy remarked happily.

Brianna laughed. "Well, I'm glad to see I've bolstered your confidence."

"As a matter of fact, my confidence needs bolstering," Mandy admitted.

"Uh-oh, sounds like you took my advice. Have you and Luke broached the subject of children?" Brianna queried, her voice laced with concern.

Mandy nodded. "Luke says my ability or inability to have children has no bearing on our commitment to each other." She paused, remembering their conversation. "I hope he means what he says. I want to believe he means what he says," she stressed, "but I'm afraid if it becomes a real issue, I'll lose."

"Oh, Mandy, you must know Luke is always understanding."

"Sure. But understanding is one thing. Coping with reality, dealing with failure—"

"Failure?" Brianna interrupted. "You certainly can't view a miscarriage as failure."

"No?" Mandy forced herself to focus on Brianna's puzzled expression rather than the sudden pain old memories triggered.

"Of course not," Brianna insisted.

"Some people do. My husband did."

"Luke wouldn't."

"How can you be so sure?" Mandy demanded, her voice a quiet plea. She watched as Brianna sliced a lemon, then set the paring knife on the counter and turned to face her again.

"I know Luke. He wouldn't. He's compassionate, not judgmental."

"You may be right," Mandy conceded. "But my experience with David left it's mark. I'm not sure I could live through that type of trauma again."

"Even with Luke holding your hand?" Brianna queried.

Mandy smiled at the small dark-haired woman.

"With Luke holding my hand, I could face just about anything."

"Well, then," Brianna asserted, "there's no problem!"

"Right. We have it totally resolved," she agreed halfheartedly. "Don't you wish we really could solve problems that easily? And, speaking of problems, Brianna, have you discussed yours with Jess?"

She dropped a tea bag into the ceramic pot. "I told him about my brother's marriage and how hurt I was when Laura showed me the pictures. . . He seemed to understand." Her voice was quiet, controlled. "Jess usually feels what I feel," Brianna continued, gesturing for Mandy to sit at the table, then turning to pour boiling water into the teapot. "He knows, senses, when I'm upset, and responds compassionately. I tried not to make too much of my hurt, knowing he would take it to heart."

Brianna placed the cups and the lemon on the kitchen table as Mandy pulled out a chair and sat down.

"You mean you down-played the full extent of your feelings?" Mandy reached for a wedge of lemon.

"What can he do to change the past?"

"That isn't the issue. How you're feeling now, what hurts you now is."

"You're right," Brianna conceded reluctantly.

"You ought to share it *all* with him. After all, Luke swears that's the basis of the strength of your marriage."

"Luke's wrong." Brianna paused thoughtfully as she poured two cups of tea. She passed one to Mandy and met her eyes head on when she continued. "Sharing is important, but it's our love that provides the basis for our strong marriage. It's our love that makes being together and sharing our lives mean so much."

"Being with Luke means everything to me. His love, his happiness, sharing his daily life with him." She stirred her tea, thinking about the recent changes in her relationship with Luke. "We've chosen a lot for Luke's dream house."

Brianna's cup clattered against the saucer. "That's wonderful!" she exclaimed. "Exciting. Where?"

"Overlooking the water, near the shipyard. The view is magnificent. The land is rocky, partially wooded, and slopes gently toward the water. The house plans he designed are—" curling her fingers around the cup, she took a sip of hot tea "— spectacular."

"What's bothering you? Why do I get the feeling you're resisting this in some way?"

"I'm not resisting, Brianna. I want so badly for everything to be perfect for Luke. I want to see all his dreams come true, but I'm not a fairy godmother. I can't grant his wishes with the wave of a magic wand."

"But you can always be there for him when he comes home, when he needs you," Brianna suggested.

"If only that were enough," Mandy murmured.

"It's a good way to start," Brianna pointed out. "And the two of you are well on your way. You've established a firm foundation for your relationship. Just take it slowly."

"Slowly," Mandy repeated. She took another sip of tea and lowered the cup to the table. "The word 'slow' is not part of Luke MacLaren's vocabulary."

Brianna smiled, then laughed outright. "Maybe not."

"Definitely not," Mandy asserted, laughing along with her.

The sound of the front door groaning alerted the women that their private conversation was about to be interrupted. Brianna twisted in her seat to peer down the hall, and as she did Jess's presence filled the doorway.

"Caught you two laughing today. That's an improvement. Hi, Mandy." He approached her quickly, bestowing a brotherly kiss on her forehead, then turned to his diminutive wife. "Hi, babe," he murmured, pulling her close and kissing her full on the lips without regard to his audience.

"Our dinner-party preparations must be under control," he observed astutely.

"Perfectly," Brianna responded.

"Perfect, except for my jitters," Mandy added.

"Mom and Dad will love you, Mandy. You've brightened Luke's outlook on life. You've kept him from being lonely, you've introduced him to new foods and—"

"Don't even think it, Jess," Mandy threatened in a teasing tone.

"What?" Jess looked bewildered.

Brianna had a mischievous look in her blue eyes. "Ahh . . . the satin sheets," she teased.

Jess chuckled. "I'd almost forgotten about them."

"Feel free to forget them anytime. Both of you," Mandy instructed.

"But isn't that how you brightened his outlook on life and kept him from being lonely, Mandy?" Jess quipped.

"Jess!" Brianna exclaimed, obviously surprised that her husband dared to carry his teasing so far.

"That explanation would make a positive impression on your parents." Mandy tried hard to sound nonchalant.

"You're all right, Mandy. You're the best thing that ever happened to Luke. Don't worry about my parents asking personal questions. Noah and Bethany will provide constant diversions. Mom will be favorably impressed because Luke's got someone who cares enough to feed him regularly—"

"I make him help," she interrupted.

"Right. That's another point in your favor. No one tolerates a lazy MacLaren."

"Especially Mom," Brianna added.

"Listen," Mandy began. "I appreciate what you're trying to do here, but in all fairness to both of you, I'll be nervous no matter how hard you try to convince me otherwise. The notion of meeting the family rattles me. I'm not accustomed to family gatherings. I'm afraid I'll blunder badly and embarrass myself, or Luke—"

"Luke!" they exclaimed in unison.

Jess's deep laugh filled the room. "Honey," he informed her merrily, "Luke will not be embarrassed, even if you do your best to try!"

She shouldn't have worried. Jess and Brianna were right. Everything went smoothly. The evening was enjoyable and surprisingly relaxing. Luke's parents were warm, accepting people—as she'd expected from his description—and everything she'd ever dreamed a family could be.

Once again she garnered insight into the person he was. And as she watched him interact with his parents and his brother's family, she realized she cared deeply. She loved him even more than she had before.

From the time the doorbell pealed its warning, she only had one or two moments to worry and wonder. When the MacLarens entered, they brought a round of hugs and the music of the children's joyful laughter.

Mandy had been sitting on the floor playing a card game with Noah. Suddenly she was abandoned. From her viewpoint, the room was filled with their collective happiness and her expected trepidation.

Before she even blinked though, Noah was back, tugging her to her feet, urging her to "Come meet my grandma."

Libby MacLaren's warm smile and welcoming gaze chased Mandy's apprehension right away. Mandy was at ease with her even before she spoke. Her lively gray eyes were comforting.

Of course, Noah's enthusiastic, "Grandma, Grandma! This is Uncle Luke's girlfriend, Mandy. She's my friend, too. She made me cupcakes. And she plays games with me" completely eliminated any tension.

The moment the all too jubilant child stopped, Libby MacLaren touched her fingers to Mandy's arm and said, "It's so nice to meet you, Mandy. Noah has been bursting with stories. 'Uncle Luke this, Mandy that' the child's such a little dynamo, he could sell you just about anything, it seems."

Mandy laughed and hugged Noah to her. "You are so right! Maybe I should hire this little charmer and put him to work selling houses. What a boost for business!"

And then, with little more than a smile and one "Please, Grandma, please," Noah had convinced his Grandma to join their card game.

The second moment of pause hit Mandy when Luke waltzed through the door. Late.

Looking thoroughly annoyed, he handed the salad to Brianna and announced in a bone-weary voice, "I need a drink. Do you have any *strong* iced tea?"

Mandy was certain she'd stopped breathing for those few seconds before the words "iced tea" rang through the air. Then he surprised her, throwing her emotionally off balance when he tugged her into his arms and whispered, "Hi ya, Mandy mine." His lips were no less demanding than usual, despite his audience.

Noah's awed "Wow!" cooled his ardor. He repeated the child's "Wow!" and, laughing unashamedly, pulled Mandy toward the couch.

As he sat back, he rested a possessive arm around her shoulders and began a long explanation of why he was late. To everyone's amusement, he related the tale of a prospective client who was more persnickety than a half-dozen elderly spinsters combined.

"Are you going to work with this person, or suggest a good Realtor?" Mandy dared to tease as he finished.

Luke chuckled and, tracing circles on her shoulder with his index finger, said, "I hadn't thought about it, but perhaps I should find him a Realtor. I told him I'd prepare several preliminary sketches. If they aren't acceptable, we'll both have an out."

"Don't send him my way," Mandy threatened. "Not if he's as difficult as you make him sound."

"He is and I won't," he promised, kissing her again.

This kiss had been no more than a comforting brush of his lips against her forehead. But it made her realize Luke's intention to show his family her place in his life. After that, she relaxed against him and thoroughly enjoyed the evening.

As they sat in the living room Tuesday evening, Luke studied Mandy thoughtfully. She had been almost monosyllabic during dinner, and now she was engrossed in a quilting square. It seemed as if she'd withdrawn from him.

At first he suspected she was overtired from a long day at work, but after watching her covertly, he'd decided it was much more than fatigue or the pressures of her business. The look he'd detected in her eyes several times was akin to melancholy.

"You're awfully quiet tonight. What's wrong?" he asked, concern edging his voice.

She raised her eyes slowly to meet with his, staring at him for endless minutes, studying him solemnly, before she responded.

"What makes you think anything is wrong?" she challenged.

"Amanda . . . ." he threatened.

Mandy almost smiled. "Okay. I admit it. I'm down."

"Why?"

"Why?" she repeated pensively.

"Mandy. Cut the echo routine. What's wrong?"

"I suppose . . . a combination of emotions have welled up inside me . . . and are warring," she revealed, her low voice even huskier than usual.

"And what do you suppose triggered this, uh, war " he asked, trying to choose his words carefully."

"This morning I baby-sat for Noah and Bethany—" She stopped short.

Luke's eyebrows wrinkled as he puzzled over her statement and her attitude. "Noah and Bethany were a problem?"

"Oh, no, they were fascinating. Noah is perpetual motion in the shape of a boy—but you know that. And Bethany is a dear, sweet angel of a baby. Of course they weren't a problem."

"Yeah. Of course. So the problem is?" He paused, waiting for her to jump in with an explanation.

"The problem is," Mandy reported slowly, "that Brianna had an appointment with her obstetrician—"

"She's all right, isn't she?" he interrupted.

"Well, yes . . ." she hedged.

"Mandy, what's wrong?"

"I'm trying to tell you!"

"Okay. I'll be quiet. You talk."

"Apparently Brianna was concerned because this pregnancy was, er, different from her two previous pregnancies." Mandy hesitated. "You know she hasn't told anyone else—family, that is—that they're expecting again. She asked me to baby-sit because she assumed I'd ask fewer questions."

"Is Brianna all right?" Luke asked.

"She's fine. She . . . Jess went along with her this

morning." Mandy almost smiled, remembering. "You should have seen the two of them when they returned from the doctor's office. They were ecstatic—grinning and laughing like a couple of silly kids. And the way they stare at each other. . . ." her voice drifted off.

"Love struck," Luke proclaimed.

"Exactly," she agreed.

"And you can't deal with the fact that my brother is besotted by his beautiful wife and vice versa?" Luke quizzed.

"No, no, no, *no!*"

Mandy smiled, actually smiled. He was sure it was the first time all evening.

"I admit I'm amazed at how strong their relationship is," she revealed, "but I certainly don't have problems dealing with it. It's good to see two people so much in love, so openly loving to each other. They have it all. I—"

"They deserve it all," he emphasized. "Every little scrap of time together, every happiness that comes their way. They've more than earned it."

As he spoke, Mandy stared pointedly at him. He read the look and muttered, "Yeah . . . Back on track. The doctor had good news?"

She nodded, lowering her eyes, suddenly feeling frozen in place. She took a long, slow, sustaining breath. "Brianna is carrying twins." Her husky voice was barely audible.

"Twins," Luke repeated reverently. "Wow!"

"A double blessing." Mandy voiced her deepest thoughts out loud.

"One they deserve," he reminded her. "They want a large family, which is probably why they were so pleased when they returned this morning."

"Strange how happiness comes to some . . . and not to others. Strange how some people seem to get just what they want . . . and others always have to work for every little scrap.''

''Jealous?''

She raised her eyes to meet his.

''No,'' she denied. ''I'm not jealous of Jess and Brianna.''

''Have you read Brianna's first book?''

A puzzled expression clouded Amanda's lovely face. ''Brianna's book?''

Luke smoothed his mustache with his thumb and forefinger. ''Yeah. Brianna's book.''

Mandy shook her head in denial and confusion.

''Our Brianna is a special lady. A very private, special lady. I guess we all protect her, guard her privacy so much it's second nature. The den in that big old house of theirs—the deep-blue room lined with shelves of books—is Brianna's private sanctum. Jess passes it off as *their* den, but he's camouflaging his lady's retreat. Brianna is an author. Brianna Dugan.''

Amanda's eyebrows rose just a tad and a soft, quiet ''ohhh'' escaped her mouth. ''I didn't realize. . . . I mean,'' she stammered, ''no one told me.''

''An oversight, Mandy mine,'' he apologized. ''Have you read *A Lonely Road* or *Full Pockets*?''

''No,'' she admitted. ''But don't you have copies of each in your bookcase?''

''Yeah,'' he drawled. ''I sure do. Brianna has a knack for revealing her demons with her pen and camouflaging herself and her loved ones in the weave of her tales. Read her books, Mandy. Get to know Brianna the way the rest of us do. Then you'll agree anything that brings her happiness is well-deserved.''

''I don't begrudge them their happiness, Luke. I never said that.''

''I know,'' he insisted. ''But I know what you didn't say.''

"What?" Amanda's brows came together as she puzzled over his comment.

Luke extended his large hand toward her, then ran the tip of one long finger lightly along her jawbone. "What you didn't say, lady, is how deeply this morning's incident troubled you. What you didn't say is how much you wished it were you having those babies."

Her eyes flew open wide, her jaw slackened. She was too stunned to speak.

"Wanna come over here into my arms, darling?" Luke coaxed. "I think we need to have a serious discussion about this."

Troubled aquamarine eyes pleaded with his. But she relented quickly, moving into the comfort of his arms, where she knew she would find at least temporary relief from her private torment.

"How can you be so sure of my thoughts?" she breathed.

"How could I not know your thoughts, sweet angel?" he countered. "Tonight you've been quiet and withdrawn, unlike the Amanda Burke I live with. I knew something was troubling you. It took forever for you to get around to it." He paused thoughtfully.

"You fell apart when you learned of Brianna's pregnancy. You had to struggle to tell me the truth about your own pregnancy. But I know how much you love children, Mandy. I've seen you with Noah and Bethany. If I'm not mistaken, you probably shared in Brianna's joy this morning. Then, as the day wore on, you started feeling, as you say, down. Am I right?"

"You are." She shook her head curtly. "I really am thrilled about the twins. . . ." Her voice trailed off.

"Yeah. I can see how thrilled you are," he teased.

For long moments Luke studied the woman in his arms. Her masks were gone again. She was permitting him a glimpse of her inner self, allowing him to share a small part of the pain she tried so hard to hide.

"How do you feel about gambling, Amanda?" he asked, his low rumble filled with an unaccustomed seriousness.

"Gambling?" she echoed in confusion.

"Gambling," he emphasized. "Taking risks . . ." he whispered, pausing momentarily to search her face for reaction. "Having babies?"

The room was silent. And except for the even rhythm of their breathing, there was no movement.

He waited. Her answer was important. *She* was important to him. Therefore, he would wait.

At last he felt her body relax slightly. She expelled a long breath of air. "I, um, want to have a baby, Luke," she whispered.

"So do I, sweet angel. So do I," he murmured, drawing her against him. "Ah, Mandy mine, I'm right here with you. I always will be."

"Oh, Luke," she breathed. "I'm frightened and worried. . . ."

Gently he wiped a tear from her face. "And ready? Are you ready in spite of being frightened and worried?"

Her reply was a faint "Yes."

"We'll be in this together." He ran a finger down her cheek. "We'll share frightened and worried. All right?"

She nodded several times. "All right."

An invisible weight lifted from his shoulders. "Good. Together we may be strong enough to fence with the demons from your past and defeat them."

"I wish—"

He cut her off with a kiss he couldn't withhold another minute.

"You know what I like best about our discussions, Mandy mine?"

"What?" she asked absently.

"I like what comes afterward!" he declared, hugging her.

Mandy couldn't help but smile at his enthusiasm. "Making love," she whispered.

"Making love," Luke groaned as he covered her mouth with his own. "Private celebrations." He kissed her again. "Wanna have a fancy dinner celebration tomorrow night?" he managed to ask between impassioned kisses.

"Private. Now," she responded.

"Both," he insisted, sweeping her off her feet to carry her to their bed with the silken sheets.

ELEVEN

Luke was nervous. He'd spent the day getting the necessary papers and permits to begin building their home. But as much of a headache as he considered the legalities, they were not the source of the tension mounting inside him.

He was worried about his celebration with Mandy. He'd made plans to meet her at a very exclusive restaurant on the water. When he'd made the reservation, he had requested a secluded table for two. He'd ordered white roses to be sent to the restaurant and red roses to be sent to Burke and Benson. He wanted tonight to be perfect.

Yet, even after he had completed the preparations, he worried. He'd assumed so much with Mandy right from the start. He had taken her home and made love to her with little thought for her feelings. He had depended on her friendship and warmth countless times, needing her to be there for him. He'd assumed she wouldn't mind his company and had dropped in unannounced time after time until, without discussing the matter, they were as good as sharing her apartment.

And when he had broached the subject of moving in, he'd given her no time at all to consider the matter.

From there his assumptions, as he thought of them, had snowballed. He wanted to build his dream house and share it with her. He had assumed she'd want the same. And so they had discussed the matter. Mandy had agreed—had even helped to choose the site. In a few months, their dream house would be a reality.

Now his latest assumption. For a moment he silently chastised himself for using the same kind of steamroller tactics his older brother was best known for. He'd assumed Mandy wanted a child as much as he did, mostly because she was so touched by his nieces and nephew.

He wasn't out and out demanding to have a baby, but he felt a little as if he had pushed her, as if he had perhaps rushed the issue. Trouble was, he didn't like standing in the wings watching his brother and sister. He wanted to be an active participant. He wanted his own family. When backed into a corner, Amanda had revealed that she did, too. And yet Luke couldn't help feeling guilty that he'd forced her to admit her innermost feelings.

Tonight he would be honest with her. Not that he hadn't been in the past. But now he wanted her to know exactly what he was feeling. He wanted his feelings out in the open and hoped she would lay hers before him, too. They would discuss, as they always did, but he hoped with more depth and honesty. He was committed, heart and soul, to loving this woman. Although he assumed she knew that, tonight he would make very certain she did.

Mandy savored the rich, fluffy chocolate as it melted in her mouth. Chocolate Seduction, it was called. Luke had ordered a large slice for each of them.

She had tried off and on over the course of their

dinner to study him, but each time she'd glanced his way, he'd been staring at her.

Finally she couldn't stand it any longer. "Something wrong, MacLaren?" she asked.

"Not a thing. This dessert is perfect," he replied, grinning. "Aptly named. Only you are sweeter, Mandy mine."

Her fork froze in midair. In private, Luke MacLaren was overtly affectionate, aggressive. In public, he was, most often, as reserved about his feelings as his elder brother. Mandy was dumbfounded. She knew she was staring.

"What's wrong?" he queried.

"I was wondering that myself, Luke. You're acting peculiar."

"Yeah?" he questioned, looking puzzled. "Peculiar?"

Mandy chuckled. "Moonstruck," she whispered, her smile bright, her eyes dancing.

"Yeah, moonstruck." He sighed and shook his head, as if in disbelief. "I am, you know," he revealed.

"You are . . ." Mandy frowned, not understanding. "Moonstruck?"

"Yeah." Reaching across the table, he enfolded her slender hand within his own, then stared at their hands pressed together. Slowly, very slowly, he raised his eyes to hers.

"I love you, Mandy," he declared, his voice reverent. "I love you so much, sweet angel, I can't imagine what my life would be without you. I never thought . . . I never knew you could need another person's love as much as I need yours." He released a long ragged breath. "Truly moonstruck," he whispered. His fingers rubbed gently, tenderly against hers.

"I love you, too." Her husky voice was like a lover's caress, arousing him without conscious effort.

He swallowed, straining to control the wealth of overpowering emotions he felt.

"Have I been guilty of asking too much too soon, Amanda? Have I pushed too hard for what I want? Have I unintentionally ignored what you want?"

"Guilt, Luke?" she queried. "Why do you feel guilty? You've no reason to. You've been considerate of me and of my feelings. As far as my wants go . . . don't you know, darling Luke, that *you* are all I want and all I need?"

"Ah, Mandy," he breathed. "I feel as if I'm not giving you enough, as if all I'm doing is taking—and taking without asking."

"Silly," she scolded. "You always give. You always share. You rarely take without asking. And everything I give you, I give freely."

"Your love."

"Yes, my love. It's all yours, freely given. No refunds accepted."

"I've taken it without giving in return," he confessed.

"Nooo! You've given me love, Luke, without recognizing it," she explained.

"Yeah? Maybe I have," he conceded.

"Believe me, you have. You aren't a taker."

"Do you feel pressured by my . . . desires?"

"Your *physical* desires, MacLaren?" she teased.

He smiled, appearing oddly chagrined. "No, Mandy. I'm confident my physical desires aren't too much for you. I meant my . . . my dreams—" He broke off suddenly.

"Your dreams," Mandy repeated. "*Our* home and *our* family?"

"Yeah," he admitted, realizing she had answered simply by placing the emphasis on "our."

"Shared dreams," she informed him.

"Yeah. *Shared* dreams." He lifted his green eyes to

share more than dreams, locking them with hers for endless moments, making silent promises, silent schemes for their future.

"Will you marry me, Mandy?" he asked, his low rumble vibrant with emotion. "Will you be my wife and share my dreams?"

When she smiled, happiness radiated not only from her bright eyes, but from all of her. "I will, Luke," she responded softly.

"Yeah?"

"Yeah, MacLaren," she assured him. "And you can relax now. I've said yes."

"Are you willing to wait until Drew can get home for our wedding?"

"Of course, Luke. Stop worrying."

"Are you willing to postpone making babies until after the wedding?"

"Luke!" she exclaimed. "No wonder you've been so tense tonight. All these questions. Of course we'll wait, as long as you aren't going to stop practicing, too."

"Hell no, lady," he quickly returned. "As a matter of fact, don't you think it's about time we went home to have our practice session for today?"

"Indeed I do," Mandy agreed. "Indeed I do."

Amanda awakened and within seconds realized the sounds and smells from the kitchen must have penetrated her sleep. The other side of the bed was empty, but obviously Luke wasn't far away. She heard the low, tinny sound of music from the radio. She heard flatware and dishes being rattled. And she couldn't help but smell the coffee and bacon. She smiled to herself, half pleased, half amused by Luke's overt efforts to prove his capabilities in their partnership.

When she stretched lazily on the satin sheets, her

naked body slid over the cool fabric, reminding her of last night. She and Luke had truly celebrated their engagement. She closed her eyes, remembering Luke's concern, Luke's tenderness, his passion . . . his love. He'd given it all to her before. But never, never had it been as beautiful as last night.

Maybe it was finally hearing him profess his love for her outright—although she had known deep down it had been there for months, unspoken. Or maybe it was the precision planning of every perfect detail of his proposal, from the roses he'd sent her at work, down to the tiny little box he'd left under her pillow.

She smiled dreamily as she lifted her left hand and gazed at the intricate engagement ring she now wore. Diamonds and sapphires. Tasteful yet spectacular. What was it Luke had said? "It's you, sweet angel, all cool light and blue fire. Sparkling, Dazzling. Yet delicate and feminine, like you."

She sighed deeply.

And just when I thought nothing could be any better, Mandy mused as she inhaled the delicious smells emanating from the kitchen, *now he's cooking for me*.

"Delight" was not a strong enough word to describe the way she felt. She felt loved—truly loved. At the moment the realization struck her, tears sprang to her eyes, filled them, spilled over, and streamed down her face.

"What s wrong? Why are you crying, sweet angel?" Luke's low voice carried the weight of his concern.

As she glanced up, he came to sit beside her on the bed. He reached out one hand, gently wiping the tears from her cheek.

"Aren't you happy?" he whispered. A trace of agony vibrated through his words.

"I'm very happy. I love you, Luke," she murmured, wrapping her slender arms around his neck. "I love you so much and you love me, and I'm crying like a silly fool because I'm very, very happy.''

"Lord, Mandy." He swallowed hard as he pulled her close. "I thought something was wrong."

"Nothing's wrong. Everything is perfect. Except that I woke up all alone," she teased.

"Yeah, well, I can explain that," he began.

"There's no need to explain. I can smell the coffee and the bacon. Luke, thank you—"

The words were abruptly cut off as his mouth covered hers, masterfully taking, possessing, and at the same time, sharing.

"Breakfast in bed, Amanda?" he whispered.

"Will anything burn if we have dessert first?"

Pulling her with him as he flopped back on the mattress, he sighed contentedly. "No. I turned off everything in the kitchen. It's all ready. I've even fixed the tray." He pressed his lips to her forehead. "Only thing cooking now, Mandy mine, is me."

"Dessert first?" she whispered.

"Wouldn't have it any other way." He hugged her closer and began to feast on her ripe lips.

Later that day, Luke and Mandy drove out to their lot overlooking the sea. Luke had grabbed a bottle of wine from the refrigerator and two glasses from the cupboard. Mandy, witnessing this, quoted "A jug of wine, a loaf of bread—and thou beside me. . . ." And in no time they had assembled a simple, impromptu picnic.

Now they sat on a blanket in the meadow, watching the waves beat along the shore below the bluff. Luke studied Mandy's face while she sipped her wine.

"Is something bothering you?" he queried. "You seem to drift away from me every now and then. Your eyes . . . Have I done something to upset you?"

"No," she was quick to assure him. "Oh no, no, darling Luke." She reached to lovingly caress his cheek. "I was remembering past demons."

"Again?" His forehead wrinkled as he puzzled over her comment. "I thought we'd finally slain the last of those guys." Grinning wickedly, he captured her hand in his, holding it close to his lips.

Her eyes danced with amusement and with love. She gave him a faint, sheepish smile.

"Well, you see, MacLaren," she offered, trying to sound casual, "I thought I had buried a few deep enough so that I wouldn't have to face them again, but—" she licked her lips "—I don't think I can forget them, or dismiss them, quite so easily."

As he listened, Luke studied her carefully, intently— viewing her tension, as well as feeling and hearing it.

She raised her eyes to meet his head on. "I don't want my demons or my secrets to come between us. I guess I ought to tell you about them."

"Yeah. Why don't you snuggle over here next to me," he suggested. "Isn't that the established procedure for these deep, soul-searching sessions? Let me hold you, Mandy mine. Let me help you forget. . . ." he whispered.

Mandy moved quickly into his open arms. And after seemingly endless minutes in an ardent embrace, he released her mouth, yet kept her wrapped securely within his arms.

"Spill it, Mandy," he ordered, a low rumbling chuckle following his command.

Stalling, she licked her lips again, this time to savor the taste of him. Then she swallowed hard, trying to muster the courage to speak—to bare the deepest secrets of her soul to the man who professed to love her.

"Time has a way of healing scars," she said, her low, husky voice barely audible.

"Love erases them," Luke declared.

"Has my love for you done that, Luke? Has love erased the scars for you?"

"Yeah," he whispered against the white cloud of hair where his chin rested.

"Maybe someday I'll reach that point, too," she speculated. "I guess that's what made me cry this morning. All at once I realized how much you love me and what a glorious feeling of well-being your love brings. I felt healed and oh so happy."

She paused, remembering. "And the feeling just grows, with each minute it intensifies. Yet, there's this leftover demon inside me, creating the tiniest smidgen of doubt. I don't want that demon there, Luke. I want everything to be perfect for you. But that's not possible with the little demon in the background. Oh, I can try to hide it, suppress it, but I *don't want anything* spoiling what we've found, what we have together."

"So we'll slay the little monster, Mandy mine," Luke offered gently. "Together."

A slow, wistful smile spread across her face. "If only it were that easy."

"Tell me," he coaxed.

She nodded her head. Luke watched the blond hair bob up and down, felt it's silkiness against his chin, and concentrated on what she was saying.

"My divorce was .. . nasty."

"Yeah," he ground out. "Tell me something I don't already know, lady."

"Yeah," she echoed. "David wanted a family. And I did, too. After Ben died, I tried hard to please him, to be the perfect wife—"

"And here you are again, trying to be perfect for me, aren't you?"

"I guess I am, Luke. But it's different with you. You let me be me. With David I was always trying to be what he wanted me to be. And I never could be. I never managed to be the wife he wanted. When I couldn't give him the family he expected us to have . . . he left.''

"Whoa. Back up," Luke interrupted suddenly. "You know what you just said? You said he left—"

"Because I miscarried our child," she finished for him.

Luke turned her in his arms, staring deep into her eyes, questioning, searching, yet silently telling her he cared.

"I want the details," he demanded solemnly. "I need to know exactly how that bastard—"

"Shhh," she breathed, covering his mouth with one slender finger. She swallowed hard. "That's what I'm trying to tell you. But, believe me, Luke, you don't need all the details.''

"Amanda . . ." he threatened.

She met his eyes and held his intense gaze as she spoke. "Shortly after I lost the baby, David came to my hospital room and informed me in his own selfish style that he didn't want to be married to a woman who couldn't—'' She broke off, drawing in a long breath, fighting against the pain that never seemed to go away. "Who couldn't even perform the natural womanly function of reproduction.''

Mandy saw the storm clouds building in Luke's eyes and hurried on before he had too much time to react.

"It's over, Luke. It's behind me. It's history," she stated emphatically.

"Yeah," he growled. "But it, *he,* is the reason you are so damned afraid to have our babies!''

"But you're not David, you're Luke. And you aren't like him. *You* wouldn't leave. You would stay and love me no matter what," she asserted quietly.

"I'll always love you, no matter what," he murmured, hugging her to him. "Did it take you all this time to figure that out, Mandy?"

She sighed ever so slowly and felt the built-up tension leave her body. A delightful current of contentment replaced it as she relaxed against him. "Maybe it did, Luke. Maybe it did."

"Well, lady—" he brushed light kisses along her ear, "—do we have any more demons to slay?"

"I think not" was her happy response as she peeked up at him.

"Whew! I'm glad that's over. Slaying demons is a tough job. I feel like I've been on a damned roller coaster .. . or maybe it was the rack."

"I know the feeling," she returned.

Although her tone was teasing, he didn't miss the serious undercurrent. For several minutes he merely held her, kept her close to him, letting his love wash over her, hoping his feeling of contentment was shared. And hoping, too, that they'd seen the last of their demons, put their unwanted insecurities behind them. He wanted his open declaration of love to be a beginning, like their engagement, of the best phase of their relationship. He wanted everything with and for Mandy.

"Wanna move our blanket behind those rocks over there?" he asked suddenly.

"This is a beautiful spot. Why move?" Her husky voice wrapped around him like a velvet glove.

"It'll be even more beautiful over there, Mandy, mine," he promised, his eyes now dancing with desire.

"Yeah," she agreed, realizing his intent. "I'm sure it will be beautiful over there, MacLaren. So what are you waiting for? If you move your cute buns, I'll carry the blanket."

He rose slowly, his eyes boring into Mandy's as she busied herself moving the remains of their picnic.

"Now," he whispered, extending his large hand toward her.

"And always, Luke." she smiled, placing her hand in his.

Luke dropped his next surprise the following evening. They were having dinner—one of their cozy, impromptu dinners in bed.

"I wrote to Drew this morning requesting his presence at our nuptials."

"In those words?"

"Yeah," Luke laughed. "He knows what nuptials are."

"I wasn't questioning Drew's intelligence. It's yours I'm not so sure about."

"Yeah?" He screwed up his face. "I thought we'd agreed to wait until he could come home?"

"We did, Luke. But why were you so formal?"

"Oh, that," Luke explained. "Jess and Drew have this thing about classy blondes—"

"Oh, that," Mandy mocked, laughing. "I've heard all about it. It's probably genetic. Brianna thinks Noah likes blondes, too."

"Yeah, sure. The kid is only six."

"But already has the MacLaren charm," Mandy pointed out.

"He's a kid, Mandy."

"He's a dynamo, Luke."

"Yeah," he drawled, "and I love him like crazy. And Bethany and Megan and Molly, too."

"Drew had better hurry. I don't think you can wait much longer."

He didn't respond, just stared at her solemnly, studying her.

"What's wrong?" she asked when she felt the intensity of his stare and looked up at him.

"I can wait, Amanda," he stated, his low voice quiet. "We have all those kids to love. I'll wait as long as it takes. We aren't competing with big brother. This is *our* life, not anyone else's. And if we can't have babies, we'll have each other. That's what's important. You. Me. Our life. Our love. I love *you*, Mandy. I love the woman you are right now. I always will. It doesn't matter to me what you can or can't give me. My love for you is unconditional. I love you just because you're you, Mandy mine."

"I love you, too, darling," she proclaimed softly.

"Yeah . . ." Filled with contentment, he couldn't keep from smiling. "Why don't we plan the wedding while we're waiting to hear from Drew?"

"It doesn't take much planning to phone the minister, Luke."

"You want it simple?"

"Very simple," she declared. "Just family and a few close friends. And no hoopla."

Luke chuckled. "No hoopla? Okay, Mandy mine. Have it your way. But *I* want a honeymoon."

"Oh, you do, do you?" she returned. "Intimate or with hoopla?"

"Both."

"You can't have both."

"Sure. I want a special romantic interlude planned to suit our needs."

"So far it sounds good," she allowed.

"You'll need to buy more of those provocative little bits of lingerie to help set the scene."

"No problem." She smiled at the mischievous glint in his eyes.

"I'll need to get the plane tickets, make the reservations . . ."

"Plane? To where?"

"How about the islands? We can rent a place on

the beach, sail, skin-dive, make love," he suggested, watching her.

"Sounds wonderful," she murmured.

"Intimate enough?"

"Yes. But, Luke, you'll need to pin Drew down to a definite day and time, especially if you're planning to go to such great lengths for our honeymoon."

"I indicated that much when I wrote to him. Told him he ought to take some leave. We'll see."

"The islands, MacLaren?" she teased, her eyes twinkling playfully. "You're a romantic. . . ."

"Guess I am," he agreed. "Why don't you slide that lovely body over here into my arms and let me show you just how much of a romantic I am, Mandy mine."

_____ TWELVE _____

Luke stood stiffly, nervously, at the edge of the garden beneath the towering pines. As he gazed out at his parents' yard, he was aware on one level of the peaceful rustle of warm autumn breezes, and on another level, of the comforting presence of his family seated in rows of perfectly lined chairs.

Touching a finger to the white rose in the lapel of his pearl grey tuxedo, he scanned the faces of his loved ones. They were all there—his parents, each and every one of his brothers and sisters, his nephew, and his nieces. He drew in a deep breath and said a prayer of gratitude, wanting to share this day, this event with them. He didn't want his wedding to be private. He wanted it to be a family celebration of the love he and Mandy had found.

As soft strains of harp music floated through the air, Luke's eyes sought his bride. He watched her glide through the arch leading into the garden, pass the hydrangea resplendent in pastel hues, then step into a ray of sunshine beaming through the lofty pines. For that moment she appeared captured by the sunbeam. She

215

looked ethereal, his own earthly angel. He blinked back tears that unexpectedly clouded his vision. Now he understood fully the tears of joy he'd seen in Mandy's eyes when they became engaged.

She moved gracefully along the white runner spread across the lawn. Each step brought her closer to him, closer to the moment she would become his wife.

Luke drew in a fortifying breath. Mandy was dressed in pale pink satin. She'd kept the gown a secret, saying only that she wanted to surprise him. He was more than surprised, he was awed by her serene allure. The satin clung to her, covered her from her slender shoulders to her shapely ankles. He had never seen her look more feminine, more elegant, or more desirable.

While his eyes feasted on his bride, impatience nearly overcame him. He wanted to rush forward, draw her into his arms, and tell her all the things that he was feeling in his heart. But propriety demanded that he stand there and endure the seemingly endless wait, watching as she moved forward much too slowly to suit him.

And then she was within touching distance. Murmuring "Sweet angel," under his breath, he reached out eagerly and grasped her hand in his.

Her radiant smile was his undoing. He stared down at her, feeling overpowered with so much emotion that he suddenly went numb.

Mandy's softly whispered "Luke," accompanied by the gentle squeeze of her hand brought him back into focus. He reminded himself that they'd planned a simple, brief ceremony. It would be over soon and he could hold her forever afterward. But right now he needed, wanted to exchange vows with her.

Gazing at Mandy, he saw his joy mirrored in her eyes. He clasped her hand more tightly and felt her respond in kind. His anxiety ebbed, replaced by a contentment that spread slowly throughout his body. He knew Mandy sensed the change. For a fleeting moment, a lighthearted expression danced across her face, then she winked at him.

He couldn't suppress his spontaneous grin. She knew him so well. In her own way, she was sending him silent promises that went beyond the words of any formal ceremony. Promises, commitment, communication. That's what this was all about. Not just publicly proclaiming their love for and devotion to each other, but vowing to listen, to understand, to share—no matter what the future held.

As he recited the words that would forever bind him to the woman he loved, Luke watched Mandy—the sparkle in her eyes, the glow of her smile, the way her white-blond hair glistened in the sunlight, the sheen of the pale pink satin dress. He breathed in the fragrance of her softly-scented perfume and felt the caress of the autumn breeze as if it were bestowing approval on their union.

Then it was Mandy's turn. As she took his left hand in both of hers, Luke felt her tremble for the first time. But her husky voice held steady when she slipped the circle of gold around his finger and began, "With this ring, I thee wed . . ."

One evening six months later, while Luke was tied up with a client, Mandy took a stroll around their new home. The evening was filled with damp, gentle sea breezes and the sounds of waves spilling onto the rocks below the bluff. Their perfect lot overlooking the water was now dominated by the large modern structure Luke had designed. Though the house stood splendidly for all to see, it did not detract from the beauty of the land. Mandy knew that was Luke's gift—a melding of the creation of man and the magnificence of nature.

The huge, two-story, octagonal building was constructed of wood and glass, with a wide deck surrounding the first floor and a smaller deck off the large master bedroom. It was open, airy, casual, and suited them perfectly.

Eventually, Mandy drifted upstairs and onto their private balcony. She took a deep breath, inhaling the essence of the approaching night. She felt loved, contented, and at peace.

As she leaned against the rail of the deck, she exhaled slowly. She didn't even flinch at the gentle touch of Luke's large, warm hand on her back.

"What's a nice girl like you doing out here all alone?"

"I'm waiting for a friend."

"Yeah? We're friends, aren't we, Mandy mine?"

She nodded. "Friends . . . lovers . . . husband and wife . . ." she whispered.

"Yeah," he murmured, as he drew her close. "Husband . . ." his arms tightened around her possessively, "and wife."

"Luke," Mandy began, her voice like velvet in the night air. "I saw David today."

"Yeah?" he responded curiously. The presence of Mandy's ex-husband was not a threat. Luke was sure of his wife and of her feelings.

"He hasn't changed at all," she revealed. "Still the same self-centered David Burke I married way back when."

"You spoke with him?" Luke inquired, gently tracing a path from her shoulder toward her fingertips.

Mandy nodded again. "I was in the toy department shopping for a birthday gift for Noah. David suddenly materialized out of nowhere. What a shock! One minute I was concentrating on the toys on the shelf in front of me, trying my darnedest to select the perfect gift for our nephew the dynamo, and the next, I was face to face with David! And not only David, but David and a stroller full of little girl!"

"Oh, Mandy," he murmured.

"No, Luke," she countered. "I don't need sympathy. Let me explain. I hadn't realized David had married again, hadn't given it any thought actually. But that doesn't matter. David's got the most adorable daughter. For the first few moments I was utterly envious." Mandy sighed, remembering. "The moments passed quickly as I listened to David whining about how disappointed he was that he didn't have a son, how much he wanted a son, and how he intended to keep trying until he got one."

Mandy paused, grinning in the moonlight.

"Incredible, isn't it, that a man can be so selfish, so self-centered, that he can't even see what he already has."

"Yeah," Luke muttered. "Incredible."

"But don't you see, Luke," Mandy continued. "David and his darling daughter made me take a closer look at my life, at what I have . . ." She turned to face her husband, her eyes shining with excitement, with pure joy.

"David will *never* be happy. He'll *never* have the feelings of contentment and total happiness that I have," she declared. "I have your love, Luke. It's all I need. You're my whole life. Nothing, *nothing* is more important than what we share. Nothing, Luke," she emphasized quietly. "I love you very much."

He stared down into her sparkling eyes and grinned.

"Yeah," he drawled, pulling her closer. "I love you, too, sweet angel. Maybe it took me a long time to say the words, maybe I didn't express my feelings as well as I could have, but you know they're here," he whispered, placing her hand on his chest. "Here in my heart.'' Luke raised her hand to his lips, tenderly pressing a kiss into her palm.

"You know, when Maggie left me I was devastated. I never imagined a future without her. She was my life and all I wanted was to marry her.''

He paused suddenly, sucking in a great gulp of air.

"Toward the end of that relationship,'' he continued solemnly, "I was obsessed with settling down. I thought I'd given Maggie enough breathing space. I thought I'd always considered her point of view. But maybe I smothered her with my demands.

"It hurt so damn much when she chose her career over our future. I spent nights alone wanting her, needing her, and knowing deep inside she didn't want or need me. My heart kept hoping. I had such a hard time accepting reality. It hurt to hear Maggie say she loved me, but love wasn't enough.'' Luke gripped Mandy's hand.

"Love isn't enough, sweet angel. You need trust, understanding, communication . . . much more than love alone.'' He chuckled suddenly, unexpectedly. "More than the excitement of a quick, casual roll in the hay.''

Mandy smiled, too, remembering their first encounter.

"Losing Maggie,'' he continued, "was difficult. I loved her, Mandy. A part of me will always love her. We shared so much. I never thought the void she left in my life would be filled.'' He sighed deeply.

"Thank God, I was wrong. Just look what I've found.'' The tenor of his voice could only be described as blissful. "My own lovely, sweet angel who is all I could ever want and more. So much more . . .'' Luke's words were muffled as his mouth pressed against Mandy's. Their kiss held promises of love now and forever after, of a love so strong even time could not dim its bright flame. In that kiss Luke and Mandy felt the oneness of their souls and a blanket of peacefulness enveloped them.

"Yeah," Luke murmured against the warmth of Mandy's lips. "We didn't need to honeymoon in paradise."

"We didn't?" Mandy whispered quizzically.

"No, lady," Luke replied. "It's here. Paradise is wherever *you* are."

"Yeah," Mandy drawled in a perfect imitation of her husband. "Our own private paradise . . ."

SHARE THE FUN . . .
SHARE YOUR NEW-FOUND TREASURE!!

You don't want to let your new books out of your sight? That's okay. Your friends can get their own. Order below.

No. 59 13 DAYS OF LUCK by Lacey Dancer
Author Pippa Weldon finds her real-life hero in Joshua Luck.

No. 60 SARA'S ANGEL by Sharon Sala
Sara *must* get to Hawk. He's the only one who can help.

No. 61 HOME FIELD ADVANTAGE by Janice Bartlett
Marian shows John there is more to life than just professional sports.

No. 62 FOR SERVICES RENDERED by Ann Patrick
Nick's life is in perfect order until he meets Claire!

No. 63 WHERE THERE'S A WILL by Leanne Banks
Chelsea goes toe-to-toe with her new, unhappy business partner.

No. 64 YESTERDAY'S FANTASY by Pamela Macaluso
Melissa always had a crush on Morgan. Maybe dreams do come true!

No. 65 TO CATCH A LORELEI by Phyllis Houseman
Lorelei sets a trap for Daniel but gets caught in it herself.

No. 66 BACK OF BEYOND by Shirley Faye
Dani and Jesse are forced to face their true feelings for each other.
